I0572043

Also by Eric Laster
Static
The Adventures of Erasmus Twiddle

Forthcoming
Welfy Q: Hairy Days

WELFY Q.
DEEDERHOTH
MEAT PURVEYOR
WORLD SAVIOR

Praise for
Welfy Q. Deederhoth:
Meat Purveyor, World Savior

A main selection of the Independent Meat Sellers Association.
The baloney industry's Book of the Year.
On over 1,000 cafeteria workers' "best of" lists.
Winner of the We're Finicky Readers but We Like It Gold Medal.
Nominated for Outstanding Achievement with Food & Letters.
Finalist for the National Awesome Book Award.

"Dazzling! A triumph! Quite simply, the best book about people
and luncheon meats that I have ever read!"
—*The Hungry Librarians' Journal*

"Sets the new standard for the book as narrative sandwich. Packed
between the bread-like covers of *Welfy Q. Deederhoth* is a protein-rich,
well-balanced tale guaranteed to bring tears to your eyes and laughter
to your heart in equal measure. The fulfilling conclusion of this
book will certainly leave you burping with satisfaction."
—*U.S. Ate Today*

"A revelation! I wasn't sure Eric even knew how to read!"
—Mrs. Laster (the author's mother)

"It's stupid! I love it!"
—Hal Stuart (ten-year-old)

"Once in a long while a book comes along that demands to be called a
masterpiece. *Welfy Q. Deederhoth* might or might not be such a book, but
according to most teachers and librarians,
a reader could certainly do worse.
Grade: Pretty Brilliant."
—*Entertainmeat Weekly*

"I laughed very quietly but very consistently
while reading this wonderful book."
—Somebody of Reasonable Importance

"Full of humor, wisdom, and heartache, *Welfy Q. Deederhoth*
by Eric Laster features some of the most memorable characters
to come along since I can't remember when."
—*Deli Man's Quarterly*

"Proves in most entertaining fashion that food isn't just for breakfast,
brunch, lunch, dinner, supper, and snacks. Highly recommended."
—*The Cleveland Lettuce Dealer*

"You'll never look at your local sandwich-maker the same way again."
—*Vanity Sausage*

"A nicely sized book. The perfect length."
—*CheeseList* (starred review)

"Marvelous! Delightful! Irresistible! I haven't actually read it, but
everyone else I know has and that's got to count for something."
—A Lady the Author Randomly Met on the Street

"Shakespeare's stomach is growling in his grave. J.K. Rowling is like
'OMG, *Welfy Q. Deederhoth* is such a totally profound and hilarious book,
and why am I so hungry?' S.E. Hinton admits that the book eerily
parallels a time in her own life that she has never been able to satisfactorily
write about, and is thus glad that Mr. Laster did it for her.
George Lucas is ROFL. A+++++!"
—U.S. Food and Drug Administration

E 77 ST

DEEDERHOTH

ILLUSTRATIONS BY MAX GRAENITZ

OPSIMATH

Published by Opsimath Press
ISBN 978-0-9850437-8-0

Jacket and book design by doublemranch.com
Additional design by Debbie Berne Design

For Kate

DELICIOUS HAM!

TABLE OF CONTENTS

GRAMERCY
DELI
DEFINITELY NEEDS FIXING

1

IS THIRD WEEK in New York City, with only seventy-nine cents in his pocket and a stomach that hasn't known food for a day and a half, Welfy Q. Deederhoth walks block after block, hoping for something to eat. Delis, grocery stores, coffee shops, pizza places, Chinese restaurants, falafel counters, French bistros—Welfy enters all of these and more, offering to sweep and mop the floor, to clean out the basement or storage room, to dust shelves, to do any kind of work at all for a cheeseburger, slice of pepperoni pizza, egg roll, sandwich or half-sandwich, for whatever sweeping and mopping a floor, cleaning out a basement, or dusting shelves might be worth to the person in charge.

Gramercy Deli—one of New York City's last hold-outs from a bygone era of avenues lined with family-owned businesses—is little more than an oversize shoebox filled with meatstuff, cheesestuff, and other stuff. Its two aisles stock the sort of merchandise we might buy on our way home from work, when we need toilet paper or milk but don't want to visit a supermarket so gigantic it requires a GPS to navigate. Its sandwich counter offers only the most conventional of meats and cheeses—roast beef, ham, turkey, chicken; American, Swiss, cheddar. Its refrigerators house colorful regiments of only the most popular sodas, energy drinks, fruit juices, and flavored waters.

Welfy enters Gramercy Deli fearing it will be just another in a long line of unfriendly food retailers. Not needing to embarrass himself in front of more people than necessary, he decides to wait until the store is empty of customers before asking the aproned man behind the counter for work.

He pretends to be interested in the breakfast cereals. The man behind the counter flicks a glance his way. Welfy feigns interest in the canned vegetables. Again the counterman glances at him.

Probably thinks I'm going to steal something.

Welfy is no longer sure how he looks to other people. He sometimes glimpses his reflection in a window, and although he never thinks he looks too bad, maybe he's just getting used to looking bad—which is to say, grubby. Maybe grubby doesn't seem so grubby to him anymore, while to others his grubbiness is obvious—evidence that he has to steal in order to survive.

And if I don't get work soon . . .

A bell above the door signals the last customer's departure. Determined not to let past rejections show in tone or demeanor, Welfy approaches the man behind the counter.

"Are you the manager?" he asks.

"Manager, owner, stockboy, janitor, bookkeeper," the man answers, gesturing vaguely, "you name it."

This is already better than Welfy expected. The way the man's been training a wary eye on him, he had braced himself to hear that he'll find no help in Gramercy Deli, whatever he wants. The optimism that's been dammed up within his heart, stoppered by hardships and disappointments—an optimism Welfy thought he no longer possessed—floods through him.

"If you need any kind of work done," he says, "mopping your floor or any kind of cleaning up, things like that, I can do it for you. All I ask is that if you approve of the job I do, you give me something to eat. Whatever you think is fair."

This is where the man is supposed to say he can mop his own floor, thank you very much. But Gramercy's manager/owner/stockboy/janitor/bookkeeper funnels his lips a thoughtful moment, then waves for Welfy to follow him to an alcove at the back of the store, where he keeps a broom, mop, bucket of rags and cleaning supplies.

"You might want to put that on," he says, indicating an old deli apron splotched with stains that hangs from a hook.

Welfy's not about to argue. He ties on the apron and for the next several hours cleans as he has never cleaned in his life, bending low to sweep under the bottommost shelves, mopping neglected corners, and thoroughly dusting merchandise. He wants Gramercy's metal shelves to gleam, and gleam they do—as much as decades-old metal shelves can gleam. He wants Gramercy's floor to shine, and shine it does—as much as linoleum scuffed and dirtied by thousands of pavement-battered shoes can shine.

The afternoon passes into night and Gramercy's manager/owner/stockboy/janitor/bookkeeper checks Welfy's work from time to time. But he says nothing until half an hour after closing, when Welfy—carrying a ham sandwich wrapped in wax paper, bag of Doritos, and sixteen-ounce bottle of Evian, but already worried about how he might secure food tomorrow—is about to leave.

"My name's Morton, by the way," the man says.

"Welfy. Welfy Deederhoth."

Stupid. Should have given a phony name.

"Really?"

"Uh huh."

"Well . . . good job today, Mr. Deederhoth. You can come back tomorrow if you want and I'll see what I can find for you to do. I open at six."

Welfy nods, noncommittal, and hurries out to the street. Around the corner, he rips his sandwich from its bag and stands in the middle of the sidewalk, swallowing greedy mouthfuls of ham and bread and lettuce.

He's heard people say that food tastes better after you haven't eaten in a while, but not at first it doesn't. His Adam's apple bobbing like a piston, Welfy eats too quickly to taste anything.

Gonna throw up if I keep attacking the sandwich like this.

A kid can't go a day and a half without food—the three days before that eating only scraps scavenged from garbage cans—and then stuff his face. Welfy knows from experience: the stomach will rebel.

He forces himself to stop eating and wrap up what remains. He should be happy. He's got food, after all. And he's been offered employment, which means more food. He's just not sure he can accept the job since he told Morton his real name.

Maybe talk the situation over with Harlan.

Why not? Harlan's been living on the streets forever and is super smart. If anyone can help Welfy figure out what to do, it's Harlan. But when he gets to the East 77th Street subway station, Harlan isn't under the uptown platform, as expected, and Welfy doesn't much feel like waiting around in case the kid shows up. The weather is warm and mild. Why not sleep outside instead of in that sooty tunnel where rats and clattering trains will wake him every hour?

Not devouring his entire ham sandwich in one go was hard, but this is way harder—leaving what's left of the sandwich for Harlan. Welfy surrounds and covers the sandwich with rocks, which he hopes will be enough to protect it from the rats.

Exiting the subway station, he walks to Central Park and beds down within sight of the 72nd Street boat pond. But sleep is impossible. He lies awake, eating the occasional Dorito and trying to convince himself that, having confessed his birth name to Morton, it will be too compromising for him to show up at Gramercy Deli in the morning. But if he doesn't, he'll have to search for work again, and he hates going from block to block, humbling himself before unsympathetic store managers who treat him like some third-class kid, as if he's asking for charity.

At 5:45 a.m. Welfy is waiting for Morton on the sidewalk outside Gramercy Deli.

And so it goes for a week—every night after closing, Morton says, "Come back tomorrow if you want and I'll see what I can find for you to do," and every night Welfy strips off the apron he wears while working, then steps to the street with a bag of Doritos, sixteen-ounce Evian, and sandwich wrapped in wax paper. Every night, beneath the platform at the 77th Street subway station, Welfy leaves half his sandwich and a note for Harlan. On alternate days he leaves the Doritos too. But he always writes the same note: that Harlan can meet him outside the 76th Street entrance to Central Park at 9:00 p.m. the following night. Harlan never appears at the park entrance, although in the 77th Street subway station, Welfy always finds the half-sandwich and Doritos gone.

That's how it is with kids like him and Harlan. Sometimes you hang around together, other times you don't.

And all week, while Harlan is off doing who knows what, Welfy sleeps alone in Central Park, usually near the boat pond or Sheep Meadow. And every night, unsure whether or not to go to Gramercy in the morning, he repeatedly wakes until, with the faintest hint of daylight in the sky, he gets up, brushes the clinging leaves and grass from his clothes, and checks the time on the electronic billboard high above Central Park South. By 5:45 every morning, Welfy is again standing outside the shuttered Gramercy Deli.

"Those the only clothes you have?" Morton asks after a week.

Welfy has been expecting this question. He's tried to keep clean, to look presentable, *normal.* He routinely washes up in the deli's bathroom, which is so tiny its walls pick fights with his elbows while he splashes water on himself and dries off with scratchy brown paper towels. Welfy's pretty sure he doesn't stink. *He* doesn't smell anything, but who knows? Maybe he's gotten used to his own stink. Still, his clothes are a problem. There is only so much he can do wearing the same clothes to work all the time. Not even the deli apron hides them, even though he puts it on as quickly as he can each morning.

"Yeah," he shrugs.

"Where are you living? Do you have a place?"

How to answer? Welfy feels like saying that he has the city, the state, the whole country.

"Parents?" Morton asks. "Or other family?"

Welfy almost runs, bolts out the door into the hustle of New York where he doesn't have to answer questions.

"What about a shelter? Don't you have anywhere you can go?"

"If I had somewhere to go, you think I'd be here?" Welfy answers, his voice more hostile than he intended.

Morton eases off. "All right, I'm not asking because I want to get into your business. You're a good worker and I have a proposition. I'll give you a roof over your head, food in your belly, and seventy-five dollars a week cash if you work here.

The days are fourteen hours long and not at all glamorous, as you already know. I wouldn't exactly call it slave labor, but you'd be cheaper than anyone else I can get. What do you say? You'd be doing me a favor and, from what I can tell, I'd be doing you one."

Welfy knows that Morton might try to lull him into complacency, might wait until he relaxes into routine and then report him to the police—a boy living alone on the streets who should be home with his family, attending school, doing all the typical kid stuff. The police will ask questions about his past—a past Welfy feels has never belonged to him but has instead been mistakenly thrust on him by whatever forces organize the universe.

"Why not?" he says to Morton, because risky as it might be, he has to take a chance.

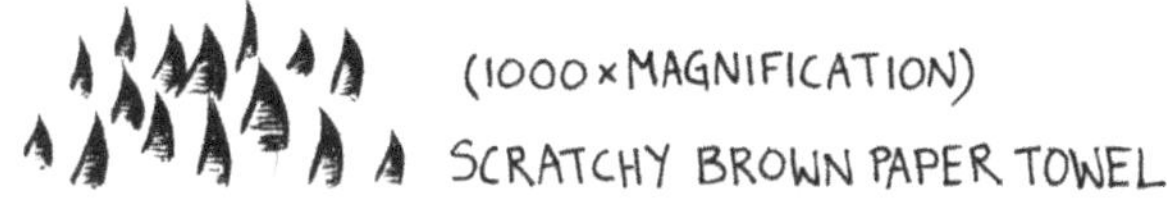

ROYAL HAIRPIN

2

ELSEWHERE.

She shouldn't be doing this—visiting the same underground stream she's visited three times already. Princess Nnnn's been told: she can have no behavioral habits that will allow enemy patrols to ambush her.

Not that her hunted, nomadic existence generally allows for habits to develop other than those of defense, such as vigilance and stealth.

And not that anyone ever wants to let the princess venture *anywhere* alone.

Which is why she deceived Prince Ffff and her uncle.

Pretending to go off as part of a reconnaissance team whose soldiers had no idea she was to accompany them, Nnnn came here, for the fourth time in as many days, to sit on the stream's damp bank, the murmuring water a soundtrack to her thoughts.

"Princess Nnnn must live," her uncle often tells her, as if speaking to another. "Being one of the last royals of the decimated Brundeedle population, it is the princess's duty to stay alive."

She must live, he means, not so much for herself but because she's a symbol of hope—for an end to Woe Time, for a future that, however faintly, might resemble the well-being and peace of the past. She's supposed to embody the resilience of the Brundeedle race.

But how can she manage such a burden if she feels bled

of all hope? To represent the fortitude of the Brundeedle race, their stubborn refusal to succumb for all time to enemy violence . . . for *that* the princess needs inner strength. And being alone for a short while somehow helps; she's able to shrug off hopelessness and despair and reinvigorate her mind, her will. Maybe why it helps has to do with *remembering*.

Because the Ceparids have annihilated everything of importance—not every building in every former city, but all literature, art, and historical archives. As if to say, *Brundeedle culture has no past, so it will have no future.*

In solitude, Princess Nnnn has quiet enough to build up a store of pre-Woe Time memories, and she strives to keep the best of Brundeedle society firmly in mind, to prevent its highest achievements from being forever forgotten. If the Ceparids are defeated, she intends to be the means by which these achievements are retrieved.

It's just that lately, instead of mentally cataloging the highpoints of Brundeedle society—its masterpieces of literature and visual art, its scientific breakthroughs—the princess has been indulging memories closer to heart and hearth.

Recollecting a banquet celebrating some historic piece of governmental legislation, she reminds herself not of the legislation's finer points so much as sees the way her father's upper cheeks pillowed when he laughed, and hears his happy voice reverberate around the dining court.

Calling to mind a literary work from the royal library—*Lfg*o Hg*bgilggoi*, say—instead of reciting an adventuresome part of the story, to be passed down to whatever posterity there might be, Princess Nnnn once again lives through those nights her mother read the work aloud to her, just the two of them in her room. She again hears the lullaby of her mother's voice and experiences the hush of impending sleep.

Something scrapes against rock behind her. Instinctively, Nnnn reaches for the Globulator at her waist.

"Yah!"

It's just Raoul.

Just Raoul? As if—husband Prince Ffff excepted—her little brother isn't everything to her!

"Blf hiciolmo," Nnnn says. *You scared me.*

Raoul's features contort and she realizes her mistake: there's enough *scary* in their lives.

"Blf hfikiaholmo," she corrects. *You surprised me.*

She doesn't want to think what might happen if Raoul lost her too—as if the loss of parents and four brothers, the cruel absence of family, isn't hers also.

Her uncle is right. Princess Nnnn must stay alive. For Raoul.

"How did you know I was here?" she asks in Brundeedle.

"It was easy. I'm an excellent spy," he says. The left side of his face quickly grimaces, relaxes: a nervous tic that started just after their parents were killed.

"Excellent spies can keep a secret, can't they?" she asks.

Raoul snorts. "I've *been* keeping it. This is your fourth time here. The soldiers everyone thinks you went with are returning to camp."

"I guess we'd better head back then."

The princess smiles—a melancholy smile that hovers at her lips while her brother says he wants to show her something.

"I've been practicing my stealth moves," he says.

Not for the first time, Nnnn wishes he weren't so eager to join the fight against the Ceparids. She and her uncle and her husband—so far, they have kept Brundeedles Raoul's age and younger from combat. But if the situation doesn't improve soon, more soldiers will be needed.

"I'll go ahead, and you follow as quietly as you can," Raoul instructs. "When you don't expect it, there I'll be. I'll detect you without you detecting me."

So Princess Nnnn waits, counting thirty Mahhahhakka, while her brother hurries down the catacomb that leads to the Brundeedle camp.

"Twenty-nine Mahhahhakka, thirty," she finishes aloud.

Leisurely pursuing Raoul, her thoughts go where they will and alight on the morning she and her brothers waited at the steps outside her parents' suite, breathing the air of jittery anticipation until the nurse emerged carrying an addition to the family—Raoul, swaddled, newly born.

The catacomb intersects another, and Princess Nnnn arrives at the crossing simultaneously with two Ceparids on patrol. Resembling some ill-considered hybrid of an outsize insect and a prehistoric reptile, Ceparids would be hideous to the princess's eye even if they weren't the enemy, and her hand is at her weapon before she remembers: Raoul, barnacled against a rock wall somewhere up ahead, waiting to impress her. He'll come running if he hears combat. She cannot risk him being wounded or worse. She can risk her own life, but not his.

Recovering from their surprise, the Ceparids aim their Globulators at the princess, but they have yet to fire when she does what no Brundeedle has done before: sets her weapon on the ground, unstraps her munitions belt and drops it, raising her arms in surrender. Although she'll never lead them to the Brundeedle encampment, not even if they torture her.

I'm going to die, she thinks. It isn't self-pity but a realistic assessment of her situation. *Right here, right now, I'm going to die.*

3

HE DAY WILL be routine until the very moment it isn't, as most days are when everything changes.

Living and working at Gramercy Deli for a week, Welfy has arranged a private space for himself at the back of the store, separated from the aisles of merchandise by a shower curtain that hangs on a clothesline. The traveler's alarm clock beeps at 5:15 a.m. and he wakes on his cot next to the cleaning supplies. He sits up and shivers, less from the cold—he sleeps fully clothed under a heap of blankets—and more to jump-start his body for the day's activities.

Welfy shuffles to the bathroom and washes his face and hands. In the deli proper, he dons his apron, switches on the lights, and sets the coffee machine to brewing. He's slicing onions and tomatoes by the time Morton cyclones in at 5:50 with the morning's supply of fresh bagels.

"I come bearing the wisdom of the heavens and bagels!"

It's Morton's typical greeting, and as always, Welfy assumes that the man doesn't mean he's brought with him the wisdom of the heavens and the wisdom of bagels. Which is what it sounds like.

But then, maybe that's *exactly* what Morton means. Welfy can't be sure. He still doesn't know much about his boss. Only that the guy spends most of his time at the deli, has an apartment somewhere on East 95th Street and a wife named Elle. Welfy figures Morton to be in his late thirties. But really, he doesn't want to know much about the man. Whatever else the past has taught him, he's learned that it's best not to be interested in the people he lives among at any given time. He's never with them for long.

"A lot of planetary activity in Aries," Morton says, distributing bagels into the appropriate bins—sesame, onion, egg, whole wheat, poppy seed.

That's another thing about Morton: he's always talking about planetary alignments, rising moons, this or that being in some "house." Welfy doesn't believe in astrological prognostications, that the motions of stars and planets billions of light years away can foretell a person's future or even influence his day-to-day. Having to listen to Morton's cosmic chatter is just part of the job, he figures, which he isn't ready to give up. Because before he can give it up, he needs a plan for what to do, where to go next.

The morning hours pass with the usual influx of customers. Welfy sometimes tends to requests for coffee, cigarettes, gum. Other times he smears toasted bagels with cream cheese or packs lox between two buttered halves of an English muffin while Morton operates the cash register. Whichever Welfy does, he can't help being aware of how well he and Morton work together—so efficient and complementary, getting done what needs to be done as if they have been a team behind that deli counter for years.

Welfy tries not to think about it: how maybe it's weird the way Morton trusts him, a kid he barely knows, with a key to the deli; trusts him not to run off in the middle of the night with armloads of food. Welfy tries not to think about how maybe it's weird the way he trusts Morton not to bring the authorities down on him, a kid who showed up one afternoon asking to work for a sandwich.

Maybe it's weird. Or maybe it's just lucky. For a change.

After the morning rush comes the usual lull. Morton sits on a stool behind the cash register, scouring the horoscope section of every New York daily and taking comprehensive notes in a red, spiral-bound notebook. Welfy checks inventory, pricing newly arrived items with the price gun he sometimes stows in his apron pocket.

Lunchtime brings more hours of customer-related activity, with Welfy and his boss taking turns at the cash register or preparing sandwiches—tuna salad on wheat, corned beef on rye, turkey and Swiss on pumpernickel. Afternoon mellows into evening. Morton occupies himself with horoscopes and his red notebook. Welfy cleans the front windows, sweeps, mops, dusts shelves, tries to keep busy.

"Did I mention I overheard a woman telling her daughter about Si Spielgut the other night?" Morton asks.

It's the first swerve from routine, but too minor to give Welfy any hint of how different his life will be within a few short hours. He knows he doesn't have to answer the question, that Morton is just working up to what he has to say.

"Si Spielgut was once the Baloney King of New York," Morton explains. "It's not often you hear someone talking about him, which is why I remember it. This woman told her daughter, 'When Si died in 1928, only brief notices appeared in the papers; he was largely a forgotten man.' The little girl didn't understand and asked, 'Mommy, what's a forgotten man?'"

Morton laughs so hard that he has to steady himself against the counter. "Get it? It was as if the girl forgot what a forgotten man was!"

"Oh. Yeah," Welfy says, hoping his forced laughter doesn't sound too fake.

At 7:55 p.m., Morton closes out the register and tallies

up the day's receipts. Fifteen minutes later he's bundled in hat and coat, his red notebook and a quarter-pound package of freshly sliced roast beef under his arm.

"Pretty good haul today," he says, pausing at the door.

"Yeah."

Welfy looks down at his ratty Adidas, smoothing the front of his apron with sweaty hands. These moments are the most uncomfortable for him, when he senses Morton's curiosity.

"If you ever want to talk about it, Welfy, I'm a good listener. Just so you know."

"Talk about what?"

"Your family situation, why you left them."

Welfy feels blood pulse in his ears. His breathing grows shallow. "There's nothing to talk about."

He could say a lot of things at this moment. Like that he appreciates working at Gramercy Deli but he just wants to be left alone to do his job and collect his pay. Like that he never wants to talk about his so-called family situation because there's no point talking about it.

Talk changes nothing.

Chance had hacked Fate's servers and burdened him with a bogus past, a false start. All he has is the possibility of a better future, which he's now, at last, trying to program for himself.

Yeah, Welfy could say any number of these things, but he doesn't. What he *does* say, though, surprises him.

"The people I left weren't *my* family."

Morton appears as if he might pursue the subject but then decides against it. "Solar chart indicated highly unusual weather in Taurus, just so you know. G'night."

Alone, Welfy gathers together a wedge of cheddar cheese and a couple of pickles—food to put by his cot for the night.

Working at Gramercy, he no longer has to worry about getting enough food and can eat as much as he wants. Still, he feels better, less uncertain about everything, when munchables are within arm's reach.

Other people have security blankets, stuffed animals—I've got security food.

Welfy flips off all the lights except the one over his cot. About to remove his deli apron—an act signifying the official end to his workday—he notices a case of Green Giant peas he should have taken to the basement. He shoulders the peas and starts to descend the basement steps. Halfway down, he trips and lurches forward, airborne. The peas go flying, and in the second before he hits the floor, he thinks *This is it, I'm dead.*

But Welfy doesn't land on hard concrete. He lands on the soft give of dirt. And when he looks up, he sees that he isn't in the basement. He isn't in Gramercy Deli or even New York. Strange aircraft whiz through a starless sky. A bright light shines on him, momentarily blinding him, and then—

Explosions. And Welfy Q. Deederhoth is running for his life.

4

EARING ONLY THE tiny scratchings of unseen creatures, Raoul waits in the dark catacomb for his sister's approach. It's unlike Nnnn to get lost in the network of tunnels that, for too long, have made up the Brundeedles' entire world. She should have caught up to him ages ago.

Unless she's trying to trick him into revealing himself?

Raoul almost laughs. He's too good to be caught out. Even by his sister. And he'll prove it.

Keeping close to the wall, he retraces his steps to the stream, imagining that no Brundeedle, not even Prince Ffff, could be quieter, more invisible, than he is. He expects his sister to jump out at him any moment. But unwittingly, she'll reveal herself before she makes her move. The whisk of a sleeve against her bodysuit, the faintest click of ParaskinGuards—Raoul has trained himself to hear such giveaways.

He sights something on the ground up ahead, where the catacomb intersects another. He approaches with suspicion, since it could be a lure Nnnn set for him. Even after he sees his sister's Globulator and munitions belt, he still thinks *gick*.

But the Ceparid Messenger Stone changes everything. The left side of Raoul's face grimaces, relaxes, grimaces.

His mouth twists open but no sound emerges. Lurching forward, he grabs his sister's belongings and the Messenger Stone, then sprints back toward the Brundeedle encampment as fast as he can.

The silence alarms them as much as anything—Raoul's facial tic hyperactive, his twisted open mouth voicing nothing while tears rickrack down his face.

"What happened?" Prince Ffff asks in Brundeedle. "What's the matter?"

The reconnaissance team has returned—both the prince and Uncle Grrrrmmph are aware that Nnnn was never in their number. For the princess to have ventured beyond camp with none but little Raoul as escort was hardly better than if she'd sneaked off on her own.

"Where's your sister?" Grrrrmmph asks.

The question brings a cry from Raoul at last. It sirens out of him with such violence and fear, the entire Brundeedle encampment is shocked to a standstill.

Almost the entire encampment.

The prince's military advisers, Pogg and Bloob, hurry over.

Blubbering incomprehensibly, Raoul thrusts the Ceparid Messenger Stone at the prince.

"Everything with those uglies is about destruction," Bloob says, because the only way to access the contents of a Ceparid Messenger Stone is to break it.

Ffff throws the fist-size object hard at the ground. In the steam that drifts up from its fractured surface, a real-time vidcast of Princess Nnnn materializes. She's encased in a bright, sparkling prism, the beauty of which is a cruel joke. Every Brundeedle knows that the enemy has no use for prisoners. Ceparid prisms are tombs.

"NO!" Raoul yells. Fresh, angry tears spring from his eyes and he reaches for his sister, as if by rescuing her likeness he can keep her from harm.

But the steam drifts apart; the vidcast dissolves.

The prince stares at where his wife's image used to be.

Bloob and Pogg share an alarmed glance. With a discreet hand, Grrrrmmph summons a nearby soldier.

"Raoul," he says, "please go with Sook. Tell her everything you can remember of what happened. The smallest detail could be crucial."

Raoul hesitates, unsure whether he's being tricked or not.

The left side of his face contorts.

"It's okay," Prince Ffff says to him. "Go on."

With Raoul too distant to hear, Grrrrmmph says, "It's a trap."

"Yes." The prince checks that his munitions belt is fully stocked, his Globulators filled to maximum.

"It's the only reason they have kept her alive this long."

"Yes," the prince says again.

"Ffff, let me deal with this," Bloob offers. "It's been almost a whole rising of the Yugmuffin moon since I've gotten to annihilate a Ceparid."

The prince seems not to hear, and the others do not say what is most on their minds: that the Brundeedles cannot afford to lose both princess and prince. It is of course devastating enough that Nnnn has been captured, but for the prince to undertake what is very likely a fatal mission . . .

"It is no less irresponsible for you to go," Grrrrmmph tries, "than it was for Princess Nnnn to leave camp alone whenever the mood overcame her."

"Irresponsible?" the prince scoffs. "What does this word mean when responsibilities we are too young to bear—all of us except you, uncle—have been thrust upon us? Nnnn, me, Bloob, even Pogg—we don't always do what's right or best. We rail against our circumstances in small ways, the only ways left to us. By sneaking off alone when it's safer to be always in company, as the princess has done. By risking bodily harm in military training, as Bloob and I have done. And by ignoring your advice, wise Grrrrmmph, who are experienced enough to know what's best and to always act accordingly. I am painfully aware of Nnnn's import to the Brundeedle population. But not being of royal blood, I am less necessary. I neither expect nor want soldiers to accompany me; the dangers are too great to justify it."

Bloob raises his hand. "Yes?" Grrrrmmph asks.

"Why wouldn't the Ceparids just follow the princess back here instead of taking her? What if they tracked Raoul and know where we are right now?"

"We need to break camp," Pogg says.

"Ready!"

Ffff and Grrrrmmph, Bloob and Pogg—all turn to see Raoul weighted down with a munitions belt and holding a Globulator in each hand. His face is puffy from crying.

"Who allowed him these weapons?" Grrrrmmph asks.

"If *you're* going, *I'm* going," Raoul says to the prince. "I should not have left her by herself."

The prince kneels in front of his brother-in-law, to try and explain why he must go alone. Raoul, he knows, is as willful and stubborn as Nnnn—perhaps even as himself—and the youngster might have to be restrained, because convincing him to stay could take some time.

Which the princess doesn't have.

5

AIRCRAFT SWARM OVERHEAD. Searchlights illuminate a landscape of charred, blasted buildings and craggy towers. Cockpit-mounted cannons shoot what look like squirts of ketchup.

Except it can't be ketchup.

Because ketchup doesn't explode and this stuff explodes on impact with everything it hits, with freestanding walls and the rusted hulls of vehicles never seen on Earth—claw-treaded vehicles of reptilian menace.

Welfy dodges the missiles, zigzagging over the unfamiliar terrain, arms up over his head as if this can somehow keep him from annihilation.

The deadly not-ketchup hails down, exploding closer and closer and—

Welfy dives for cover behind what appears to be a dumpster. He huddles there, catching his breath. Is this the future? Some alternate universe? One second he's lugging Green Giant peas to the basement of a New York City deli and the next he's being targeted, shot at, hunted?

Not possible. I'm dreaming.

If he dreams that he slaps his dream-self to wake up, will it actually wake him? Welfy tries it, slaps his right cheek with an open palm.

The white heat of a searchlight finds him. The ground not ten feet away erupts—a molten red spew that rises and falls in an umbrella pattern.

Something resembling a helicopter, but all sharp angles, crystalline, with no visible propeller and absolutely silent in flight, appears above and emits a cloud.

Poison gas, Welfy thinks.

The cloud floats toward him, disintegrating everything in its path.

Again on his feet, he sprints, streams of not-ketchup angling toward him from pursuing aircraft.

Welfy knows that he doesn't have to run serpentine—cutting first one way and then another to avoid being shot. He's played enough video games to know that it's difficult for all but the most expert marksmen to hit a moving target. The best thing he can do is run as fast as he's able, taking the shortest route to safety.

Except he can't stop himself; he cuts and weaves.

It requires serious discipline and presence of mind to run in a straight line when someone or *something* is really trying to kill you.

If I'm not dreaming . . .

Just a week earlier, he'd have thought he was hallucinating from hunger. But not now, not after he's had three full meals a day for seven straight days.

A building looms in front of him. Welfy stumbles toward it with tired legs, crashes through a first-floor window and hurtles down through blackness, down and down and down.

He lands in a thick, glutinous substance—a.k.a. goo.

He tries to sit up, has trouble because this is pretty sticky goo, but finally manages. He looks around. Four walls, a ceiling: it could be any room he might find on Earth.

Except for the goo.

And the large, glowing prism floating in the corner. Inside the obelisk-shaped prism is the kind of girl Welfy might have chatted up and given a free Coke if she'd walked into Gramercy Deli—slender, liquid-eyed, with wavy brown hair hanging past her shoulders. She's probably about his age, a year or two older at most.

"Hurry, you must hurry!" she says. Her English is stilted, as if she learned it in a classroom. "You must use the key."

"What key?" Welfy asks, but before the girl can answer, a satellite the size of a basketball and resembling a human eye—neon red pupil, visible circuits for veins—drops down the shaft and into the room. The satellite hovers in midair, pivots toward Welfy and the girl, and then rockets back up the shaft. "I don't know what's going on," Welfy says to the girl, "or who you are—"

"Nnnn."

"What?"

"My name is Nnnn," the girl says. "Princess Nnnn of the Brundeedle race."

"Okay, well . . . Nnnn? Something somewhere has gone kind of wrong, 'cause I don't know anything about a key or what that giant eye wanted or why someone's shooting ketchup lasers—"

"Ceparids."

Sepa-what?

"Ceparids. Shooting Rador-Blood," Nnnn explains.

"Uh huh. Listen," Welfy says, "my being here is kind of, um . . . traumatic, you know? Am I supposed to act like you and these Sepa-whatevers aren't in my head? 'Cause no offense, but I'm not really sure I believe in the existence of alien worlds or extraterrestrials, even though—yeah, I'm aware that in this scenario *I* might be the extraterrestrial, in which case . . ." Welfy raises his voice for anyone who might be listening, " . . . I come in peace!" Again addressing Princess

Nnnn, he says: "But I mean, these Sepa-whatevers seem like they want me dead, and—"

Clicketyclick, clacketyclickclicket: the sound of robot-fingers typing fast on a computer keyboard. *Clickclacketyclickclick*: of steel-legged roaches scaling down the shaft. *Clackclicketyclick*. Whatever is making the sound, it's getting closer.

"Hurry!" Nnnn says.

A creature, the likes of which Welfy has never imagined, emerges from the shaft: one-and-a-half times his own height; languid-limbed, as if its bones are made of muscle; with rough, spiny skin, quicksilver eyes protruding from its head, and a gleaming toothy mouth that resembles the front grill of an eighteen-wheeler. The Ceparid has trouble establishing its footing in the goo but lets rip a spray of Rador-Blood from what, in the nanosecond Welfy has to notice its existence, he mistakes for some sort of wearable sculpture: a curlicue of carbon graphite strapped to the creature's wrist.

Welfy ducks, pivots, somehow manages not to get hit.

"Your apron pocket!" Nnnn yells. "Reach into your apron pocket!"

"My—?"

It's the first Welfy remembers. *I'm wearing my deli apron.* He swivels, rears, miraculously avoids getting killed by Rador-Blood as he fumbles in the pocket at the front of his apron, pulls out—

A salami.

A squirt of Rador-Blood blasts the goo at his feet, splattering him with the stuff.

Another Ceparid drops from the shaft, a sculptural weapon strapped to its wrist.

"Your apron pocket!" Nnnn yells.

"I did!"

Welfy wings the salami at the second Ceparid, whose weapon condemns it to oblivion. Welfy again reaches into his apron pocket, this time pulls out a sculptural gun of his own.

"So now what do I—?"

A glob of Rador-Blood hits the wall next to his head, the force of the detonation knocking him flat in the goo. He tries to regain his feet but the goo feels stronger somehow, more binding, in this part of the room.

Stepping toward Welfy, the Ceparids seem to swagger, as if lording their impending victory over him. One of them makes a horrible screeching noise.

Is that . . . is he . . . laughing?

So here's one way to put an end to his dream or hallucination or whatever this is. Welfy can die. But if he dies in a dream, does he die in real life? Hasn't he heard that somewhere? Or is it that he can't imagine himself dying in a dream because he doesn't know what it feels like to be dead?

About to find out!

Twisting and flailing, Welfy frantically struggles to free himself, but it's no use. The Ceparids lift their weapons, both of them screeching in merciless glee.

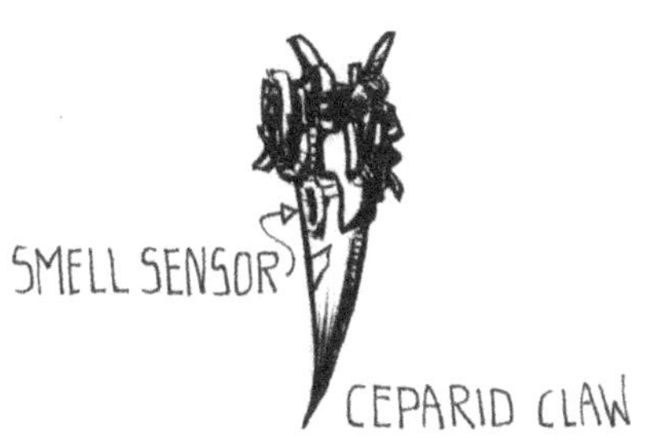

6

ELPLESS IN HER prism, Princess Nnnn can only watch as the Ceparids aim their weapons at her would-be rescuer.

Frustrated, hoping to blast the sticky stuff restraining him, Welfy triggers his sculptural Globulator. Too freaked out to aim, he shoots wild, sending Rador-Blood all around the room until he at last manages to scrabble free, stands.

"Holy . . ."

The two Ceparids are toast.

Clickclacketyclick, clickclacketyclicket: more Ceparids are descending the shaft.

"The key!" Princess Nnnn says. "Hurry!"

A recess in the wall contains a pulsating glow. Welfy maneuvers through the goo to reach it, with each step sure that his feet will get stuck and that he'll be unable to move when the next Ceparids attack. But he's wrong—thankfully wrong—because here he is, at the two-by-two square indentation in the wall, taking hold of a light-throbbing crystal, fitting it into a slot at the base of the prism that holds Princess Nnnn.

The prism vanishes.

Princess Nnnn falls into the goo. But it's as if she's been trained to cope with this type of sticky stuff, because as if there is no sticky stuff at all, she's immediately on her feet, ripping a panel from the wall, a panel Welfy hadn't even noticed, and beyond which he sees nothing but soggy blackness.

"Follow me," the princess says, crawling into the hole.

It doesn't look promising.

A Ceparid drops from the shaft. Streams of Rador-Blood angle toward Welfy. He returns fire and somehow manages to put an end to the enemy.

"Wait up!"

He scrambles after the princess, sliding down a slime-wet tunnel through the darkest dark with hardly time to think *gross* before he's jettisoned into an underground passage. He tumbles, propels himself upright and follows Nnnn, his shoes making sucking noises on the mossy ground. The princess is fast and he has trouble keeping pace with her, feels her long hair whisk against his face and is tempted to reach out and grab it, to let her pull him, he's that ready to quit all this running, Ceparids or not.

"You said you're a princess, right?" he breathes. "So that means those things back there are part of some dark rebel force?"

"Not exactly. I am a princess, yes, but when the moons of Pyron last aligned with our planet, the Ceparids took power and forced my race underground. Now we are the rebels and they are overlords of the galaxy. They have annihilated all other races and only a few hundred of my kind are left. I was being used as bait to trap them."

"You think we could . . . I don't know, maybe slow down a little? All this running . . ."

Princess Nnnn says nothing, runs swift and hard.

"Just in case this might actually be happening, which I seriously doubt, you think you could tell me what galaxy this is? Or maybe what planet I'm on?"

Still, Princess Nnnn says nothing.

"Can you at least tell me what year this is?"

"The year of Zu. You should talk less. We have a long run ahead of us before we reach the base. You will need your breath."

"Yeah, breath," Welfy says. He could use a little breath. His chest burns. His legs ache. It's even getting to the point where he has forgotten what it's like not to run. "What's to stop those Sepa-guys from following us?" he asks. "Nothing."

A loud *flump* sounds, akin to a space shuttle re-entering the Earth's atmosphere. It's followed by a whistling that grows increasingly louder as a spiked sphere cannonballs up behind them, pulling loose rocks and debris toward itself.

"Down!" Nnnn shouts. "And hold on to something! Anything!"

Welfy splays himself flat on his stomach, grips what he hopes are large, secure boulders embedded firmly in the ground. A hot, pulling sensation courses along his backside from heels to head, and he struggles to keep his body from lifting off the ground, not sure how much longer he can hold on, but—

The sphere cannonballs past.

Welfy's clothes are singed, smoking in parts, but he's fine, relatively speaking—no burns.

"Sticky Orble," Princess Nnnn explains. "In flight, objects stick to it until . . ."

The ground trembles from a blast up ahead. Rocks and dirt shake free of the solid earth surrounding Welfy, the tunnel threatening collapse.

" . . . it explodes."

"Now would be a pretty good time for me to wake up at Gramercy," Welfy says, "or even to find myself walking New York streets on an empty stomach, looking for food. I wouldn't mind those things *at all*."

The princess either doesn't hear or doesn't understand. Up

and running again, she leads Welfy down a second passage, a third and a fourth. Hurrying through an amphitheatre-like grotto, they're ambushed by Ceparids armed with gleaming, metallic weapons.

Surrounded, Welfy aims his Globulator first at one Ceparid and then another. But he has to give up; bends over, hands on his thighs, and catches his breath.

The Ceparids move in. The leader speaks:

"Blf cio foamu ˘jfago gxo cmmlbcmio, kiamiohh."

"Cm a? Hl hliib," the princess says. "Blf hxlfjlmg xceo cflfigolmo." She whispers to Welfy: "Your apron pocket."

"Blf cio iauxg," the Ceparid leader says. "Do cio gll gxlfux-grfj, dcmgamu blf cml blfi xfhfcml gl lao gluogxoi."

"Do hgiaeo gl lahckklamg blf!" Nnnn returns.

Keeping an eye on the Ceparids, Welfy eases a hand down into his apron pocket and—

"Aha!" He tries to look threatening as he holds aloft a sandwich roll. "One more step and I'll drop it!" he warns.

The Ceparids halt their advance.

"What?" Welfy says, because Princess Nnnn is frowning at him. "You think I'm used to this stuff? I'm just some kid who works in a deli!" He digs in his apron pocket with one hand, waves the roll at the Ceparids with the other. "I'll drop it! I mean it!"

"Fiamu mo gxcg hcmldaix iljj," the Ceparid leader says.

The Ceparids once again begin to move in, weapons held at the ready.

"What am I supposed to do with *this*?" Welfy asks, pulling a radiant cube from his apron pocket.

Princess Nnnn grabs the weapon and hurls it toward the far wall. It explodes into a giant firecube which tumbles toward them, engulfing squealing and frantic Ceparids.

Nnnn snatches the Globulator from Welfy and blasts at the ground around them: a large, encircling O.

The firecube rumbles closer and closer.

The floor gives way, collapses inward from Nnnn's shooting, and she and Welfy fall through the opening and splash into a subterranean river.

Fire rages out of the caved-in floor above—fire that seems to be stalking them. Welfy and the princess bob along with the river's current, the fire coming up fast at their backs.

"Forget what planet this is, okay?" Welfy says. "Just tell me where there's a portal or whatever, something I walk through and it'll take me back to Earth."

"I know of no portal." Princess Nnnn glances at the fast-approaching fire. "Take a deep breath and follow me."

She drops under the river's surface.

"Not like I have a better option," Welfy mumbles, and sucking air deep into his lungs, he dives underwater, swimming through the depths with Princess Nnnn as the fire above roils past.

7

"REALLY, I THINK I should be getting back now."
Soaked, Welfy's clothes and apron hang heavy as he and the princess trudge through yet another underground passage. "Earth. You've heard of it, right? I mean, you're speaking English, a language pretty common on Earth, so you must've heard of it. And how'd you know about the weirdness with my apron? Although, I guess . . . if I've made you up, the answer's pretty obvious."

Princess Nnnn slogs on, silent.

Welfy stops. "I'm not going anywhere until you tell me how I get out of this galaxy or universe or whatever it is."

The princess turns to him, serious. "You are The One my great-grandfather spoke of: a denizen of Earth wearing a dirty apron who falls down a shaft and lands in sticky goo to lead the Brundeedle race out of Woe Time. It was my great-grandfather who made us learn this curious language. Many hours of boring study. He mentioned this planet, Earth."

"Your great-grandfather?"

"Yes. I need your help. Many innocent Brundeedles need your help."

"But I just told you—"

Princess Nnnn abruptly turns away. "Here we are."

The archway seems to form out of nowhere, as if conjured by the princess's words *here we are*. It leads into a cavern spacious enough to house two football fields, the ceiling stippled with stalactites and at least three stories above Welfy's head.

He stands with the princess on a natural balcony formation in the cavern wall. On the floor below: a temporary settlement hundreds strong, with young children huddled around supplies, boys cooking, clustered girls speaking an alien tongue in low, serious tones. All of them are the same age as Welfy or younger, and appear no different from him—physically the same as anyone he might meet on Earth.

"Gxoio hxo ah!"

A boy—to Welfy's eye, about eight years old—catches sight of the princess and breaks away from a serious-faced teen kneeling in front of him. Nnnn maneuvers swiftly down the rough slope to the main floor and embraces the boy, who wets her with his tears. Brundeedles gather around, chattering excitedly. Sliding and skidding down after Nnnn, Welfy can't understand a word of what's being said, but he doesn't have to be a student of this alien tongue to figure out that the princess's return is a miraculous surprise.

The crowd parts as four Brundeedles approach the princess—an elderly gentleman in flowing robes and three males approximately Welfy's age, one of them the serious-faced teen who'd been kneeling in front of the young boy.

Princess Nnnn hugs each of the newcomers and spends a long minute in a three-way embrace with the eight-year-old and the serious-faced teen. Then, holding the boy lovingly at her side, she sweeps a look over those gathered round and launches into a breathless monologue. Whatever she's saying, Welfy knows it has something to do with him because Brundeedles keep turning his way. He feels kind of stupid, just standing here while aliens eyeball him, and as Nnnn drops silent, he feels not only stupid but uneasy because now every Brundeedle without exception is looking at him and they've got him surrounded.

Number one reason why I'd rather not be in this future world or wherever I am: always either running for my life or surrounded by aliens.

"So . . . hey," he says, trying to be cool.

"I am Grrrrmmph, Princess Nnnn's uncle," says the elderly Brundeedle, the sole adult in the whole Brundeedle camp as far as Welfy can tell.

"Uh, Welfy. Welfy Deederhoth."

Grrrrmmph puts a thumb to the tip of his nose, wiggles his fingers. "Oooooeee! Bock bock bock!"

Not that it will help him feel any less stupid, but Welfy puts a thumb to the tip of his nose, wiggles his fingers. "Oooooee? And . . . bock bock bock?"

"Nnnn informs us that she owes her freedom to you," Grrrrmmph says. "On behalf of her friends and the entire Brundeedle population, I want to thank you for ensuring the princess's safe return. You must be an uncommonly brave and formidable soldier."

"Yeah, not really," Welfy says.

"Most of us have apparently been under a false impression," Grrrrmmph continues. "We thought the time for a prophesied savior had long passed."

"Uh huh, well actually, I don't know anything about a prophesied savior, and anyway, you're looking at me, yeah, but," Welfy gestures at his surroundings, "I'm still trying to believe that none of this actually exists. I bet I can put my hand right through you if I think about it hard enough."

Welfy reaches out, hoping that his hand will pass through Grrrrmmph, but his fingers jab the gray-haired alien in the chest.

"You annihilated a ton of Ceparids from what the princess just told us," says a fidgety Brundeedle in Grrrrmmph's company. "Broke into their outpost and took her right out from under them. That's pretty impressive. I'm impressed anyway. I'm Bloob," he flaps a hand at the Brundeedle next to him, who's been as still and reserved as he himself has been otherwise, "head of the troops along with Pogg here, and let me be the first to say, we could use a soldier like you to kick some Ceparid butt."

"Yes," says Pogg. "Although there are some among us who doubt the prophecy of an Earthling in a dirty apron being the savior of our race, by rescuing Princess Nnnn, you have proven your courage and skills in combat, which would be valuable to us."

"Your fingers are very strong," Grrrrmmph agrees, rubbing the spot on his chest where Welfy poked him. "I have no doubt you would be of tremendous assistance. But of course it's your choice whether to fight with us or not."

"My great-grandfather prophesied that The One would be a just creature," says Princess Nnnn, "a creature of principle. I know it's no choice at all for such a one."

Welfy's eyes make the rounds—Grrrrmmph, Bloob, Pogg, Princess Nnnn, the eight-year-old boy gripping her hand. How could they possibly want him?

"Listen," he says, "you all seem, you know, pretty nice, and I'm sure you have a worthy cause. But even assuming this whole savior thing is true, no way *I'm* the prophesied one. It's just not possible 'cause . . ."

Grrrrmmph, Bloob, Pogg, and the princess grow restless—clear their throats, look off in various directions. Only the serious-faced Brundeedle who'd approached with Grrrrmmph, and who has yet to speak, appears to be listening.

" . . . what I'm saying is," Welfy goes on, "since I somehow don't seem to be imagining all this, then there's been a mistake. I mean, where I come from, I've barely been able to save *myself*, never mind an entire race. And like I already told Princess Nnnn, I don't know the first thing about weapons or combat, and . . ."

No one's listening and Welfy finishes lamely:

" . . . and I work in a deli, putting together bread and meat and . . . you know, sometimes lettuce."

The serious-faced Brundeedle steps close to Welfy, almost on his toes, and finally speaks. "So you are the one who comes from another realm to rescue fair Princess Nnnn of the Brundeedles? You are the lone soldier who defeats an entire platoon of Ceparids? You think you're special?"

"Please, Ffff. Not now," Grrrrmmph begs.

"Yeah," says Bloob, "take it easy."

"He only just arrived," Pogg tries.

"Enough!" To Welfy, the peeved Brundeedle says: "I am Prince Ffff. I have annihilated whole fleets of Ceparids by myself and will die for my race if necessary. Of course I'm relieved to have the princess returned to us—relieved and thankful—but I think perhaps it wasn't courage that motivated you to rescue her. I believe it was something else." Prince Ffff leans toward Welfy, challenging, and nods toward Nnnn. "You think she's pretty? You'd like to sniggle her, perhaps?"

"To—?"

Prince Ffff grabs Nnnn and kisses her, then glares at Welfy as if to say *You see who sniggles Princess Nnnn!* and stomps off.

The others stand around, embarrassed. "Don't mind him," Grrrrmmph says. "He gets jealous easily," says Bloob.

"Been rather uptight because of the war," Pogg admits, squinting at the far wall as if he sees something invisible to everyone else. "Shhh. Do you hear that?"

Welfy hears only the bustle of surrounding Brundeedles.

"That is the sound of the marmadillion casting his long shadow over our future. We have already waited too long and must break camp as quickly as possible." Pogg hurries away.

Nobody bothers to tell Welfy what a marmadillion is or why he should care about its long shadow. Which is probably a good thing. Grrrrmmph puts a kind hand on his shoulder.

"Get some rest, Welfy Deederhoth. I am pleased you have chosen to join us in our fight for justice. We will say more of our plans later."

The elderly one is gone before Welfy can utter a word.

Bloob, excited and happy, picks up a good-size rock. "See this?" he asks.

Welfy has no chance to answer; Bloob tosses the rock into the air and headbutts it to pieces as it falls.

"That's what we do to Ceparids around here, am I right?"

Bloob gives Welfy a wide grin, a friendly punch on the arm, and follows Grrrrmmph. Only Princess Nnnn and the eight-year-old remain.

"This is my brother," Nnnn says, introducing the boy. "His name is Raoul."

"Really?" Welfy asks. "*Raoul?*"

"Gxcmg*h rli iohifamu mb hahgoi," the youngster says.

"He's thanking you," Princess Nnnn explains.

"Ll mlg jog cmblmo hgocj xoi cucam."

"He asks that you please not let the enemy abduct me again."

"Hey," Welfy says, "I hope nobody ever gets abducted again, by Ceparids or anything else, but it's not like I have control over what other aliens do. Right now, I don't exactly feel like I have control over what *I* do."

The flatline of Raoul's mouth, the defiant stare interrupted by the facial tic: it's as if the boy is daring Welfy to disappoint him, to let him down as so many others have.

"I won't let anyone abduct your sister again." Welfy says.

Nnnn translates, and Raoul nods, unsmiling, at Welfy.

"Let's find the prince," Nnnn says, and leads her brother toward the center of camp.

I'm alone. Could make a run for it.

True. No one is in the immediate vicinity to stop Welfy from escaping down passageways that extend from the cavern like octopus tentacles. But escape to where, exactly?

Welfy curls and uncurls the fingers that poked Grrrrmmph in the chest.

So if I'm not imagining this place . . .

He's never really thought of himself as the kind to give in to fantasy anyway, the kind who tries to escape his life through wild imaginings. Because if he was that kind of kid, he would've done it long before now, when he has a job and regular meals every day.

But the fact is, before he wound up *here*—wherever here is—Welfy's life might not have been easy, he might have resented large chunks of it, but it hasn't been the toughest in the world either. There are definitely tougher.

Like Harlan's.

REBEL ALLIANCE CHOCOLATE CHIP

8

T 8:30 P.M. in New York City, Harlan Mills—tousle-haired, with close-set brown eyes and a boxer's knobbly nose—makes his way through the lavish, expansive lobby of the Hilton hotel on Sixth Avenue. Harlan is thin, a good twelve pounds underweight according to U.S. Dept. of Health and Human Services recommendations, but he looks broad and well-built because of the clothes he's wearing: three blazers, a sweater, two T-shirts under a button-down collared shirt, and three pairs of slacks, the outermost pair held up by a belt, the others by lengths of rope tied around his waist. His Nikes are a size too large and without laces. To get them to fit, he wears four pairs of socks, each more or less falling apart.

Harlan crosses the hotel lobby, weaving past flushed, smiling tourists dressed in I♥NY sweatshirts, past business-men tipsy from hours at the hotel bar. In this crowd, hotel employees are easy to spot because of their brown uniforms and the gold nameplates pinned to their chests.

As if Harlan would ever want to know the names of any employees. He won't even make eye contact with them, although he's careful not to avoid looking at them either. Too much eye contact or too little—either might seem suspicious, and the last thing Harlan wants is to act suspicious.

Because if anyone's going to toss him out of the Hilton, it will be an employee.

He stops into the men's room, a place easily large enough

to house him in grand style, with polished chrome and marble everywhere. Harlan wets his hair at the sink and, with his fingers, plasters it close to his skull in an effort to make it look neat, combed.

"You belong," he whispers to his reflection.

He buttons his outer blazer, which might be older than he is, to judge by the frayed stitching and the shininess at the elbows and shoulders. As satisfied as he's ever going to be with his current outfit, Harlan exits the bathroom and ascends a wide, carpeted staircase to the mezzanine. He's done this hundreds of times. He just has to act like he belongs in this sprawling hotel where people can have anything they want so long as they have the money to pay for it.

A hotel employee bustles past. Harlan stiffens, but—

The employee is too intent on an errand to notice him.

He's probably worrying over nothing. Has anyone here *ever* noticed him? Cared? That's usually part of the problem. No one cares. But at the Hilton, it's a good thing.

On the mezzanine, the double doors of the Grand Ballroom are flung wide. Before Harlan even passes through them, he sees the chandeliers that resemble large fountains frozen midspray, the cloth-covered tables, the red leather-backed chairs. He enters the Ballroom, discovers it full of mingling Darth Vaders, Darth Mauls, Stormtroopers, Chewbaccas, Yodas, C-3POs, and Jar Jar Binkses. Princess Leias, Queen Amidalas, Ben Kenobis, and Lando Calrissians munch hors d'oeuvres. Han Solos and Luke Skywalkers sip cocktails.

Harlan never knows what to expect at the Hilton, but he definitely wasn't expecting this: a full-on Star Wars convention with attendees dressed as their favorite characters and the famous theme music playing over a P.A. system. On the walls: movie posters for *The Empire Strikes Back*, *The Phantom*

Menace, *Attack of the Clones*, *The Last Jedi*, and every other film in the Star Wars canon.

A man wearing a dark blue suit and Chewbacca head walks past, howls.

Darth Vader, in full Galactic Empire regalia, approaches Harlan, breathing heavily the way Darth Vader does. "I think you want Registration," he says, pointing to a table at the side of the room and sounding exactly like the *real* Darth Vader.

"Yeah, thanks," Harlan says.

He moves off toward Registration, but when he sees Vader busy trying to figure out how to eat a pig-in-a-blanket without removing his helmet, Harlan alters his course toward the buffet.

Platters galore: egg rolls, vegetable dumplings, chicken skewers, lamb kabobs, shrimp cocktail, breadsticks, French rolls, baguette slices, fruit tarts, cookies, brownies, numerous cheeses. Just about anything Harlan could ever want is here.

The trick is to not seem excited.

Harlan casually pops a shrimp into his mouth. Nearby, Boba Fett—that oh-so-cool, unfeeling bounty hunter—takes a chocolate-chip cookie from the buffet in his oh-so-cool, unfeeling bounty-hunter way, then turns to visit with other guests.

Trying to occupy as little space as possible, to will himself into invisibility, Harlan fills his pockets with food.

"Naw, I don't stay at shelters 'cause the people in charge might try to put me in a group home, and from everything I've heard, those places are like jails—people always telling you what to do and when to do it. I've been independent for too long to deal with that. Besides, you don't meet the nicest people in the world at shelters. Criminals. Crazies. People with serious mental problems, you know? There's a place for teens called SafeSpace I could go to, but it's totally depressing."

Harlan is sitting on the topmost step in one of the Hilton's stairwells. The emergency exit onto the roof, rigged with an alarm should he or anyone else shoulder it open, is at his back. Next to him: a girl dressed in a white blouse and long black skirt, her hair pulled into a ponytail. Her name is Sandra Zwerling and her socks are the cleanest, whitest socks Harlan has ever seen not still hanging on a hook in Macy's or some sporting goods store. Sandra's from the Midwest. Harlan hasn't asked exactly where. It's her first trip to New York City, he knows, and her dad is an astrophysicist in town to address the United Nations Committee on the Peaceful Uses of Outer Space.

"Where do you sleep?" Sandra asks.

"Wherever," Harlan answers. "Under subway platforms. In abandoned buildings, vacant lots, parks. I know how it sounds, but it's actually cool. Always a new and different scene. And like I said, I'm independent. I can go where I want, whenever I want. I'd rather be off the grid than inside the system any day."

He checks to see if Sandra believes this stuff. Hasn't known her long enough to tell.

"I've got this friend. Calls himself Welfy. I met him a month ago under the subway platform at East 77th Street. I usually stay away from people new to the life, but sometimes you just click with someone, you know? Like us. You and me. I don't even have to ask if you feel the connection, because I know you do."

Harlan tilts his head questioningly, to see if Sandra will deny it. She doesn't. Yeah, she believes this stuff.

"Hey, you hungry for something sweet?" he asks. He reaches into the left front pocket of his outermost coat and finds a handful of cheese cubes. "Wait a sec." He tries the right front pocket: a couple of egg rolls. In the inner pocket of his middle coat: a pig-in-a-blanket. The pockets of his three pairs of pants are filled with assorted nuts and vegetables. At last, Harlan thrusts a hand into the breast pocket of his innermost T-shirt, and—

"Aha!"

He places the item on his lap: a fudge brownie wrapped in a Star Wars napkin.

"Anyway," he goes on, carefully breaking the brownie in two, "Welfy and I hang around together sometimes, because every now and then you decide it's better to pair up for a while, till you feel like going off on your own again. First week I met Welfy, I showed him the restaurants that occasionally give away leftover food at the end of a night, food that'd be thrown out otherwise. I showed him Zaro's Bakery in Grand Central, where you can get a pocketful of free samples so long as you don't act too desperate. I never told him about the Hilton, though—these conventions with the free buffets, which is where I got this brownie. I need to keep some secrets for myself. Here."

Harlan offers half the brownie to Sandra, but she hesitates.

"It's all right," he says. "I'm reasonably well-stocked at the moment, as you saw."

"'Kay. Thanks."

She's got the cutest little shrug, Harlan thinks, as she takes the fudgy sweet from him.

"But so, what I've been getting at . . . there are people who choose a life like mine and then there are the kind who get it pushed on them. Don't ask why people choose it. Could be a million reasons. But mostly it's a choice to not be where they were before, you know? Like they wanted to get away from wherever they were and they'd take care of where to live and how to pay for food once they got away. But Welfy, the friend I've been talking about? He's an exception—not one kind or the other, but both at the same time. He's a cross between the kid who chooses the life and the kid who gets it pushed on him by crummy circumstances. He's never told me his story, but I've figured out certain parts of it from hints he's dropped. Like that he'd been bouncing around the foster care system forever before he ran away. Which would make him a kid who chose this life. Because he ran away. Understand?"

She's got the cutest little nod, Harlan thinks, watching Sandra nibble her brownie and catch the crumbs in her open palm.

"Okay, but I bet if you asked Welfy, he'd say he didn't choose this life. He'd say it was forced on him because his time in the foster system was so awful, he *had* to run away. And his believing that makes him the second kind of person, the kind who has this life pushed on him by untenable circumstances."

"Un-what?"

"Untenable. Means 'indefensible, or not able to be maintained or occupied.' I saw it in an online dictionary at the public library once. I can't help memorizing pretty much everything I read. Anyway, a lot of times rookies like Welfy have more get-up-and-go when it comes to real-world stuff, at least in the beginning. This get-up-and-go usually disappears once they've been on the street awhile. They just stop caring about what most other people care about. If they didn't already, I mean. Which a lot of times is the case and is partly why they're on the street in the first place. Welfy's get-up-and-go has him working and living at a deli. Pretty *off*, right? I mean, who lives in a deli? I've heard of people living in an apartment *over* a deli, but *in* a deli? Uh uh."

Harlan stuffs his mouth with brownie, suspects that living in a deli can't be any less *off* to someone like Sandra than sleeping under a subway platform.

"Anyway, I've stopped by his deli a couple nights this week 'cause he always gives me a sandwich. Payback for that first little while I looked after him, so I guess it's all good."

"But what . . ." Sandra says, "I mean, how . . ." She doesn't finish, afraid to offend him.

"How'd I end up homeless?" Harlan's easy attitude fades. "It's not the kind of thing I tell people when I first meet them, if ever, but like I said, I feel a connection with you, so . . ." Harlan seems unaware of it: how much his expression has clouded, his voice gone deadpan. "My parents weren't the most affectionate people you could ever meet. Their idea of nurturing their one and only son—me—involved belts and barbed wire, which is all I'm going to admit on *that* subject. I was nine years old when my dad said it was time I learned how to make my own way in this world because no one was going to do it for me. He drove me hundreds of miles away from where we lived, and in the middle of nowhere he told me to get out at the side of the road and find my way back. Then he drove off."

"That's horrible!"

Harlan tries to cover his wince with a smile. He has worked hard to persuade himself, to believe with all his might, that if no one reminds him how bad this episode in his life had been, then maybe it hadn't really been so bad.

"Anyway," he says, no longer sure if he's telling the story because Sandra asked him to or because he needs to release the pressure of it being a part of him, "it took me a few days, but I did it, I found my way back. Except when I got home— which was a rented trailer in this Columbus, Ohio trailer park—my parents were gone. They'd skipped out, owing money to everybody. I have no idea where they are, or even if they're alive. And basically, I don't care."

Harlan doesn't say what he always wishes to forget at this point in the story: that his parents got rid of him the way some people abandon an unwanted pet.

"I've stuck it out on my own ever since," he concludes.

Sandra's eyes are brimming with tears. A dangerous thing for Harlan to see, as it might make him cry. And he doesn't want that. He definitely doesn't want that.

"Let's play a game," he says, to distract himself. "You have a cell phone on you?"

"Uh huh."

"You pick any two numbers between 100 and 1,000 and multiply them together on your phone's calculator. Don't tell me what the numbers are and don't tell me the answer after you multiply them together. But once you have the answer, we'll make a bet."

Sandra, sniffling and wiping her cheeks, pushes at the buttons on her phone. "All right," she says.

"Okay, so I'll give you everything in my pockets—my whole life is in these pockets—if I can't tell you what number's showing on your phone right now. You just tell me the two numbers you multiplied together, and before you can count to three, I'll tell you the answer. If I get it wrong, you keep what's in my pockets. But if I get it right, you have to give me something from the mini bar in your room."

"I'm not going to bet you."

"Chicken."

"No, it's just . . . I shouldn't have eaten your brownie. I don't want to take anything more from you."

"I'm not worried about it," Harlan laughs, shaking off the unpleasantness of a few moments before. "C'mon, I mean it. Tell me the two numbers."

"One hundred seventy-six and 324."

"Fifty-seven thousand and twenty-four," Harlan says.

Sandra hasn't even counted past one. Her eyes widen and she subsides into silent awe, holds her phone so that Harlan can see its screen. Which displays the number 57,024.

"I'm just able to do stuff like that in my head," Harlan explains. "Don't ask me how."

Sandra's room is a junior suite with a sitting area, decorated in pastels and floral patterns. It's the most luxurious apartment Harlan has ever been in, and any other time he'd already be ransacking the mini bar, but his attention is taken up by several pairs of socks in an open suitcase at the foot of a bed. Socks so clean he'd swear they were new. It's the U.N adviser's suitcase, no doubt. Sandra notices Harlan's preoccupation, and saying not a word, she presents him with a pair of her dad's socks. Then—

"Oh, good," she says, spinning round to the door, "you'll get to meet my—"

A man in a gray pinstripe suit has barely entered the room when Harlan, wary of U.N. advisers, of well-to-do adults who probably don't want their daughters hanging out with home-less kids, runs out to the hall.

"Wait!" Sandra yells, but Harlan Mills is already in the stairway, descending flight after flight, heading for the safety of the streets.

9

SURROUNDED BY BRUNDEEDLES, momentarily alone, Welfy's feeling pretty odd—although, amazingly, his being in this alien world isn't enough to account for it. Because maybe he's not used to rubbery creatures shooting deadly not-ketchup at him, but hasn't he lived with a near-constant threat of harm for as long as he can remember? Hasn't he experienced more physical and mental discomfort than any kid should? Anger, sadness, depression—he's on a first-name basis with them. But this oddness he's feeling? It's completely unfamiliar.

Princess Nnnn, Grrrrmmph, Bloob, every Brundeedle except Prince Ffff—they're certain that they need *him*. They're *glad* he's come. And Welfy's not used to feeling welcomed, embraced.

"Ocg," Raoul urges.

Nnnn's brother has inched up to him. Shyly, pretending not to, Raoul has edged toward Welfy with phony nonchalance, as if—poof!—he just happens to find himself next to the Earthling who saved his sister. And just happens to have a bowl of murky liquid, which he sets at Welfy's feet.

"Ocg."

"What's it like?" Welfy asks.

Raoul points to the bowl, pretends to pick it up and drink its contents. The left side of his face grimaces, relaxes.

"No, not that," Welfy says. "I was wondering, um . . ."

What it's like to feel as you obviously do for your sister. To have that level of trust in a person, the kind of connection that makes you want to be with her every chance you get.

Because when you've lived in thirty-one homes in the past twenty-four months, and who knows how many homes before that? When the longest you've ever lived in one place is eleven months and you can't remember everywhere you've lived or all of the people you've lived with but are sure you wouldn't want to remember them even if you could? When, throughout your life, social workers have shown up wherever you happened to be and without warning have told you to collect your few belongings because they're taking you away to a better place, which they say as if you've just died? And when these "better places" have been group homes with cots lined up in gymnasium-size rooms, and you've never known the kids you're sleeping next to or whom to trust and so you've trusted no one? When all of this is your past, as it is Welfy's, then what Raoul feels for his sister is as alien as the Brundeedles themselves.

His question left incomplete, Welfy picks up the bowl of murky liquid, takes a sniff and—"Ugh!"—scrunches his face in disgust. Setting the Brundeedle food aside, he reaches into his apron pocket and pulls out a weapon similar to brass knuckles but with long, serrated knives that jut from the crown of each finger-hole. Funny, that he never feels the weight of weapons or anything else in his apron. If he glances into the pocket, it appears empty, ordinary. But if he reaches into the pocket without looking, it seems expansive, bottomless, his hand groping air till his fingers close on some new item—as they do now—which he lifts into the open: a knish, as if warm from an oven.

"Here," he says, offering a pinch of knish to Raoul, who's watching him, curious. "Try it."

Raoul lets the food be dropped into his palm. As if fearing

it will give him an electric shock, he puts it on his tongue, where it doesn't last half a second before he makes the intergalactic expression for *Blech!* and spits it to the ground and runs away.

"They all come to appreciate the knish eventually," a voice says. "Unless, of course, they have issues with carbohydrates."

A portly man, dressed in a deli apron and holding a squeezable plastic jar of Gulden's mustard, is floating beside Welfy.

"You're no doubt wondering who I am," the apparition says.

Welfy swallows a bite of knish. "Any other time, I'd probably be freaked by a ghost carrying a jar of mustard, but I'm stuck in an alien world where I'm supposed to be some kind of action hero. A floating, see-through guy is just a little bit of weirdness in the middle of a whole lot of other weirdness. Not trying to hurt your feelings, but unless you're going to tell me how I get back to Earth, I'm not sure I care who you are."

"But I know your name," the figure says hopefully. "Welfy Q. Deederhoth. You have to admit this is intriguing."

Welfy looks more closely at his visitor. The timing would be peculiar—a ghost from the biological family he's never known haunting him only after he's stumbled into an alien world. But peculiar seems to be the new normal, so who knows? His heart thumping nearly as fast as when he was running from Ceparids, Welfy studies the apparition for any family resemblance.

"I'm Si Spielgut, the Baloney King of New York!"

Ghostly Spielgut must want to show that this is cause for celebration: a cone-shaped party hat forms in his hand, and he promptly transfers it to his head.

"Are we related?" Welfy asks.

"We are all of us related in the family of humanity," the Baloney King answers. "And in the family of all living things throughout the cosmos—past, present, and future."

"Yeah, but by blood, I mean? Am I related to you directly?"

"Not that I am aware of."

"No, course not." Welfy points to Pogg and a few Brundeedles loading a hover-sled with provisions. "What's that over there?"

Spielgut turns toward the hover-sled, and Welfy jumps up and runs behind a boulder. But here's the Baloney King, right beside him.

"Not nice," Si says.

"I know, sorry," Welfy admits. "Could you wait here a minute? I'll be right back."

Si's face puckers with doubt.

"I promise," Welfy says.

With a reluctant nod, Si indicates that he'll wait.

As casual as a Sunday stroller, Welfy walks toward a group of Brundeedles, but midway to their hover-sled he veers sharply and suddenly left. He runs through an obstacle course of supplies and hover-sleds until he's out of sight on the opposite side of the encampment. Satisfied that he's free of ghosts with no relation to him, he bites into his knish, not having a chance to swallow a single mouthful before Si Spielgut is hovering at his side, apron-clad, mustard-carrying, angry.

"I guess there's no getting rid of you," Welfy says.

"I want to tell you something," Si frowns, massaging his temples with one hand, making a pincer of his thumb and middle finger, "although I'm no longer sure you deserve to hear it. Strange. I think I'm getting a headache."

"What's the Gulden's for?" Welfy asks.

Si stares at the mustard in his hand as if seeing it for the first time. "Finally, an important question! A query for the ages, of major significance to countless generations! Please allow me to inform you, Welfy Q. Deederhoth, that as soon as I learn the answer to this mustard question, I will pass it along to you. But enough of condiments. I want to tell you—"

"Can I have it a minute?"

Si stops, blinks, doesn't see why not. As soon as Welfy takes hold of the Gulden's, it transforms from a ghostly representation of mustard to an actual jar of the stuff. Which Welfy opens, squirting a ribbon of yellow onto his knish.

"Thanks."

He hands the mustard back to Si, and it reverts to its ghostly form.

"I'm here to give you some advice," Si says. "Let's see, what did I want to say? Ah yes, I believe it was something like a hot dog is as a hot dog does ... or no, I believe it might have been ... ach, I don't remember anymore. I definitely have a headache. Who knew an energy cluster with personality could get headaches?"

The Baloney King starts to fade, but just before disappearing, in his most disembodied voice, he intones, "Use your head, Welfy."

There are questions Welfy no longer asks himself. *Why me? What'd I do to deserve this?* Another kid in his place might petulantly wonder why he's been punished with transport to alien precincts, where his life is under constant threat and seems ripe for accosting by chubby ghosts with mustard, but Welfy does not.

"Here you are."

Bloob sends Welfy's knish flying with a kick. The knish explodes on the ground in a burst of crumbs and potato-glops.

"That's what those Ceparids are gonna look like when we're done with them, right buddy?" Bloob says, and puts an arm around Welfy. "C'mon, Grrrrmmph wants a word."

Bloob escorts Welfy to a holographic display of neon red and yellow and green blotches—an aerial map, around which Prince Ffff and Princess Nnnn are holding a strategy meeting with their advisers. Raoul is at Nnnn's side, listening intently. Welfy again finds himself the object of Prince Ffff's unfriendly stare, which makes it kind of hard to focus on what Grrrrmmmph is telling him about the Ceparids.

"Their average life span is three revolutions of the Toda sun," the elderly Brundeedle explains. "Very, very short. Only Craetella, their queen, lives a long time. No one knows quite how long. She was alive before I was born and I suspect she'll remain long after all of us unless—"

"Unless we serve her a heaping platter of death," Bloob says, brandishing a fist.

"Yes," Grrrrmmmph says. "Because her soldiers live for such a short time, she must constantly birth new ones to ensure her military power. If we prevent her from birthing these new soldiers, we put a stop to the Ceparid war machine."

"We have inserted a homing NuNu in one of her probes and will soon know her exact location," Pogg says. "Annihilating her is the only way."

"We serve her a platter of death. Buy her a forever ticket to death city." Bloob shows off what appear to be his karate moves.

Princess Nnnn points to a green smudge on the holo-map. "We know that Craetella's primary stronghold is here, somewhere in the flats of the Coringa region."

"We'll settle in a new camp," Grrrrmmmph says. "Then you, Bloob, Pogg, Ffff, and Nnnn will lead a division of our best soldiers to the region. Hopefully, with the added help of your skills and your strong fingers . . ."

"Uh, yeah," Welfy says. "Hey, how about I *don't* help lead some of your best soldiers into the Coringa region, but we say

I did? Would that work for you? Because that would totally work for me."

A tense moment of silence, then most everyone laughs—long and hearty. Raoul, imitating his elders, laughs loudest of all. Prince Ffff, however, is not amused.

"We will see if you are a better soldier than you are a comedian," he says.

A tremor ripples through the cavern, a rumble: someone or something is coming.

"We should go," Pogg says. "We've already waited too long."

Zip! The holo-map vanishes.

Brundeedles have begun to leave camp, a caravan of sleds hovering into a tunnel that leads from the cavern. Grrrrmmph, Bloob, and Pogg move off to join them. But Prince Ffff looks at Princess Nnnn.

"C mlmomg, kjocho" Nnnn says.

Rolling his eyes in disgust, Ffff removes himself some distance and waits. Welfy and Princess Nnnn stand looking at each other. Raoul watches them both.

"I'm not who you think I am," Welfy says.

"Perhaps you are not who *you* think you are."

With that, the princess takes hold of Raoul's hand, and the two of them jog over to the prince and hike into the tunnel after the others.

Maybe I'm not who I think I am? What's that supposed to mean?

Another rumble passes through the cavern.

Should probably get out of here.

Welfy starts after the Brundeedles, but not ten yards into the tunnel, he notices a strange staircase carved into the wall, a staircase leading up into darkness.

"Nnnn? Bloob?" he calls, the tunnel's reverberant depths lending a hollowness to his voice.

No response. He calls out again, but these aren't the easiest names to yell at high volume.

"Grrrrmmph? Nnnn?"

The rumbling is getting louder, more frequent. Welfy really should catch up with the Brundeedles, but there's something about this staircase.

Can't just pass it by without at least . . .

He pulls a turkey slice from his apron pocket, nearly tosses it aside.

No. Might get hungry.

Putting the turkey into a back pocket of his jeans, he reaches into his apron a second time, comes up with a nub of roast beef. Maybe it's unnecessary to keep the meat when his apron has a seemingly endless supply, but it's what Welfy does. Because what if his apron turns back into a regular apron? What if he loses it or it's stolen?

On his third try, he pulls a gleaming metallic weapon from his apron pocket—one of the weapons used by the Ceparids. His finger on its trigger, he starts up the staircase, steady, cautious, ascending one step at a time.

Darkness envelops him. Something attacks, pins his arms.

"Get off!" He tries to elbow to freedom, fighting with all of his strength until—

He bursts into the harsh fluorescent light of Gramercy Deli, holding a bottle of Windex as if it's a gun.

┌──────┐
│ **10** │
└──────┘

IT ISN'T MUCH of a staircase—nine steps rising at a fifty-degree angle—but Welfy's breathing heavily and sweating.

Thump thump, thump thump.

Nothing strange at the bottom of the steps: exposed pipes, a ratty old mop knocked to the basement floor, cans of peas lying about.

Thump thump, thump thump.

Harlan is banging on the locked front door of Gramercy Deli, trying to get Welfy's attention.

Dazed, his thoughts one big question mark, and his finger on the trigger of the Windex bottle, Welfy moves to the door—doesn't remember unlocking it a second after doing so, only knows that he must have unlocked it because here's Harlan, strutting around with his three pairs of slacks bunched above the knee, making it look as if he's wearing highwaters.

"Check 'em out," Harlan says.

Welfy kind of has other things on his mind.

"The socks," Harlan says. "Brand new. Got 'em from this girl I met at the Hilton. I stopped in there to go to the bathroom, you know? Pulled the old mental-math routine on her. Pretty nice, right? A fresh pair of socks makes all the difference sometimes."

"What day is it?" Welfy asks.

Harlan stands holding his pants bunched above the knee. "I know it's easy to forget what day it is when you're sleeping in a subway station, but here? I thought you had to keep track of that kind of thing. It's Friday, Friday night."

Welfy squirts Windex at a pack of Twinkies to make sure that what he's holding is in fact Windex and not some liquid weapon from Princess Nnnn's world. Turns out it's Windex.

"Welfy?" Harlan says. "Hey? Earth to Welfy?"

Welfy aims the Windex at a pack of Devil Dogs.

"You're acting a little out of it, Welf. Gonna tell me what's up?"

"You won't believe me."

"I don't know, I'm pretty gullible when I want to be. One thing you might not have figured out yet: when you've been on the street a long time, you'll believe lots of things most people wouldn't, especially if it'll keep your mind off the fact that you live on the street."

I have to tell somebody. No way I can keep this to myself.

Welfy takes a deep breath, a here-goes-despite-what-might-happen-type of breath, and the words come shooting out of his mouth, rapid-fire verbal pellets:

"I closed up for the night and was carrying peas down to the basement when I tripped, and I thought I was gonna bite it big-time, but when I landed I wasn't hurt at all, I was in this future-like place and rubbery aliens were trying to squirt me with what I thought was ketchup, only it wasn't ketchup, it was globby streams of Rador-Blood, which is *nothing* like ketchup."

"Uh huh," Harlan says, imagining his friend in a dry, red landscape exactly like the pictures of Mars he's seen on the free computers at the public library. He imagines Welfy looking confusedly around this dry, Martian landscape until a big, slimy, green creature appears on the scene, aims a plastic ketchup bottle at him and squeezes it. Upon which, Welfy takes off running.

"And then I met this princess," Welfy says, "and she was one of the leaders of the Brundeedles—that's what they're called—and Bloob was okay but Prince Ffff was a huge jerk."

"Yes, please go on," Harlan says, imagining Snow White and a motley assortment of dwarves, one of the dwarves laughing heartily, trying to get Welfy to yuck it up too, but Welfy is focused on a sullen dwarf who wears a golden cardboard crown and sticks out his tongue, bratty.

"They wanted me to help conquer the evil overlords of the galaxy," Welfy says, "who were these rubbery alien creatures, and I tried to tell them *no*, thought maybe I was hallucinating everything and poked this old guy Grrrrmmph in the chest . . ."

"By all means, tell me more," says Harlan, imagining Welfy surrounded by the chattering dwarves and Snow White, Welfy shaking his head *no* until an elderly man, dressed in a long robe and wizard's hat, appears and lets himself be poked in the chest.

" . . . then I was back here, holding a bottle of Windex," Welfy finishes, expecting to feel better now that he's talked about the whole thing. But he doesn't. He feels dumb, as if he's just admitted an embarrassing secret that will be used to make fun of him.

He looks at Harlan, which he's been trying not to do without admitting it to himself. The kid doesn't seem about to mock him, though. Harlan's face is compressed into a thoughtful expression.

"There's gotta be some breach of spacetime," Welfy says, "because I know it's not in my head and—"

"Why don't I go back outside and we can try this again?" Harlan suggests. "We'll start over, okay?"

Harlan steps out to the sidewalk, knocks on the front door and refuses to re-enter until Welfy, unenthused, yanks it open.

"Hiya, Welf! I hope you're having a good evening?"

"I knew you wouldn't believe me."

"What? Who said? Of course I believe you. Breach in spacetime. Ketchup that isn't ketchup. Rubber aliens and Brundeedles. Perfectly reasonable."

"I'm not making it up," Welfy says. "Trust me, I tried to prove to myself that I was. But I wasn't. I'll show you."

Welfy plunges a hand into the pocket of his deli apron, pulls out—

A floppy slice of baloney.

"I didn't think you could do it," Harlan says, "but I must admit, you've convinced me."

"You don't understand. Sometimes weapons come out. And I jabbed Grrrrmmph in the chest with my finger. I *felt* it. Look, my finger's even a little bruised." Welfy holds up an index finger, which appears perfectly fine.

"How long's that meat been in your pocket?" Harlan asks. "Got anymore?" Not waiting for answer, he checks Welfy's apron: the pocket is empty.

"How could I have been making it up, after everything?" Welfy wonders aloud.

Taking the baloney in hand, Harlan risks a bite. "Still mildly delicious," he says. Then, with his mouth full: "Listen, Welf. I'm not making any judgments here—like maybe you're stressed because the city life and all this work are getting to you. I want you to know that. I want you to know that I'm just a guy eating baloney. But let's say I came to you and started telling you the story you just told me. What would *you* think?"

Welfy knows what he'd think. He'd think Harlan needed to see a shrink. Maybe he should drop the subject for now. Until he knows more. "Some girl gave you socks?" he says.

"Yeah." Harlan again bunches his slacks above the knee, looks down admiringly. "Her name's Sandra. I had to run out on her when her dad showed up, but I might try and see her again, show her what the city has to offer in the way of culture. Which reminds me, you think you could lend me a little money?"

"'Lend' means you'll pay it back."

"Correct."

Welfy knows that the likelihood of Harlan ever paying him back is about as slim as the slimmest baloney slice. He *should* know anyway, considering the amount of money he's already "lent" the kid. If he keeps making donations to the Harlan Mills Charity Fund, he'll never save enough to move into a decent room somewhere.

"Turn around. Don't look," he says.

Harlan faces the deli's refrigerators. "Don't know why you always insist on all this secret-spy stuff."

Welfy slides a package of Huggies diapers out from under his cot. He pulls a box of Ritz crackers from amid the diapers, then removes a frozen OJ concentrate container from the box of crackers. His money is in the OJ container—a wad of mostly fives and tens. He peels off his last twenty-dollar bill and stuffs the wad back into the OJ container, which he deposits back into the Ritz box, which he again stows under his cot amid the Huggies diapers.

"Thanks," Harlan says, pocketing the twenty and lying down on Welfy's cot.

"Uh uh. You can't sleep here," Welfy says. "You'd have to be gone before Morton shows up in the morning."

But Harlan closes his eyes, his breathing already so regular that Welfy thinks he's fallen asleep. Until—

"Where'd your name come from?" Harlan asks, unmoving.

"What?"

"Skipping out on the foster care system like you did, I understand why you'd give yourself a new name, but *Welfy Deederhoth*? It sounds too made up. I'm asking why you decided on it. 'Cause it's kind of an attention-getter, Welf, which isn't generally what you want when you're on the streets. Although nobody'll actually believe it's your real name, so maybe it is a good thing."

"It's my real name."

Harlan lets the silence hang for so long that Welfy is certain he's fallen asleep this time.

"How do you know?"

"I just do," Welfy expects to hear himself say. He expects the usual urge to clamp down and reveal nothing. But neither happens. Intergalactic travel fatigue? Or is it that, having survived Ceparid aggression, answering prying questions about himself no longer seems like such a big, annoying deal?

"There was this shrink at a group home awhile ago," he says. "I wasn't even ten years old and I guess she was trying to gain my trust. She said my birth parents must've wanted my name changed when they gave me up for adoption. I'd always been Roger Steubens, but she told me my real name: Welfy Deederhoth."

"And you believed her?"

"Yeah. She let me see it in my file."

Welfy thinks he knows his friend's next question: Did the shrink tell him anything about his birth parents? But Harlan doesn't ask, and he can't decide if he's glad or disappointed.

Which is unusual. Used to be, he absolutely would have been glad.

"She didn't do me any favors," he volunteers. "I got into fights all the time 'cause I stopped using any other name. I'd be at a new school and kids would call me Roger Steubens. 'My name's Welfy Deederhoth,' I'd tell them, and they'd be like, 'Whatever you say, Roger Steubens.' I'd tell them to shut up. They'd tell me 'Welfy' was a stupid name and beat on me. Nobody ever challenged me one-on-one. It was always me versus many."

"Story of our lives," Harlan murmurs, and begins to snore.

No way Welfy's going to be able to sleep anyway, not with everything that's happened. Too anxious to sit or even stand in one place, he paces the length of the deli until, without being aware of it, he takes up position at the head of the basement steps.

Nothing out of the ordinary in the basement that he can see except the knocked-over mop, the scattered cans of peas. No hint of Princess Nnnn or her world.

"What if I charged down those steps right now?" he wonders.

NOTHING LIKE KETCHUP!

$$11$$

THE CEPARID MILITARY outpost known as EeEEecheE, located three glips from the Coringa region, is nothing to sneeze at: a network of huge, jagged structures armored with thousands of overlapping plates that resemble those found on the outer shell of armadillos. ("Squamose, meaning scaly or scale-like," Harlan might announce, were he nearby to quote from the vast databank of his memory.) The overlapping plates look as if they could be made of black steel, but that amalgam doesn't exist here, and besides, the armored skin of EeEEecheE's structures is impenetrable, whereas steel is subject to buckling and melting under extreme temperatures. The outpost's mass of architecture, with every building and tower interconnected by tubulate passageways the color of darkly tinted limousine windows, is so enormous that it makes the Empire State Building look like something constructed with an Erector Set.

Presently, the midnight sky above EeEEecheE is streaked with the lights of Ceparid aircraft as they dock in hangars or take off for parts unknown—fighters whose spinning wings resemble the number eight lying on its side, helicopter-like tracking craft, Y-wing fighters, remote-operated reconnaissance drones, infiltration rockets, plasma-powered supply blimps and shuttles, all of them silent as deep space.

In a tower whose shape is reminiscent of a giant bone pile, Ceparid space-traffic controllers hunch over holographic displays, babbling alien speak into what look like Bluetooth headsets.

On a flat strip of land stubbled with rock, and led by a drill sergeant, a fleet of Ceparids does jumping jacks, their long, lithe limbs moving in perfect sync, while Ceparids close by use posters of Prince Ffff for target practice.

And in what passes for a barracks, Ceparids lounge in half eggshell-like pods filled with a milky substance. Some Ceparids sleep in these shell-beds, others play cards or scan the latest issue of *Ceparid Eeeeeeeechch*, which, loosely translated, might mean something along the lines of *Ceparid Gazette*.

By all appearances, it's any old night at this Ceparid outpost. But not far off, not as far off as they should be, the Brundeedles are settling into their new underground encampment, staking out sleeping areas, unpacking necessities. A few Brundeedles have begun to cook meals as Raoul and his friends chase one another around the cavern, enjoying a moment of reprieve between battles, between flights from the Ceparid war machine.

"I'm saying simply, I don't like him," Prince Ffff acknowledges. He stares with unseeing eyes at Pogg, who hunches over a grid, intensely manipulating action-figures of himself and the others.

"Relax, Ffff," Bloob says. "No one's disputing that you're our leader. And you've got absolutely zero to worry about as far as Nnnn's concerned, no cause to be jealous."

"Who's jealous? I said nothing of being jealous."

"Right, you said nothing, you did nothing. C'mon, Ffff, you don't have to say it. It's obvious to everyone. Pogg, you going to back me up on this?"

Pogg knows better than to involve himself in romantic matters between the prince and princess. "Leave me out of it," he says, fiddling with his action-figures. "I'm planning our attack."

"Docjlfhb xch ml kjcio am lfi hagfcgalm," says Grrrrmmph.

"Right. Exactly," Bloob says. "That's all I'm saying. That's all I've *been* saying. Please tell him, princess."

Nnnn steps behind Prince Ffff and puts her arms around him. She does not admit what she most feels, doesn't dare in front of the others—that the arrival of the long-prophesied Earthling has lightened her burden; she is no longer the only symbol of hope for the Brundeedle's future.

Speaking softly into her husband's ear, she says, "Since you are not jealous, I don't have to tell you that you never need be, that I could love no one but you."

Only the slightest upward movement of an eyebrow suggests the prince's softening. "Welfy Deederhoth," he says. "Such a good soldier and he's lost. Why else is he not here at camp?"

"You know these maverick types like to scope things out on their own," Bloob says. "He's probably at that Ceparid base right now, counting the number of guards, noting weak points, getting the general layout of the place for our attack."

"I doubt it," Prince Ffff says, and seems about to voice more unpleasant thoughts when a scuffle diverts everyone's attention.

Raoul is playing war with one of his friends. The friend, in the role of loose-limbed Ceparid, falls from fatal fire, spasming on the cavern floor in pretended annihilation. But Raoul hardly has time to savor his victory before being attacked by two others whose wobbly movements indicate that they too are Ceparids. Splatted with imaginary Rador-Blood, mad at himself for having been caught out, Raoul crumples to the ground.

Silent witnesses of this scene, Ffff, Nnnn, and their advisers hope that it isn't an omen of things to come.

12

OU WILL CONTEND with disruptions in the early stages of an important project, but this won't prevent you from making a dazzling first impression on someone with the power to hire you or to buy what you're selling at a good price.' *Village Voice*."

It's midafternoon, the day after Welfy found himself a targeted hero in a Ceparid-ruled world, and Morton is reading from the horoscope section of every New York daily, alternating between fingertip-graying newspapers and websites he accesses on a tablet computer.

Morton does this sometimes—forces Welfy to listen to astrological nonsense whenever, as Welfy figures it, the guy thinks the information might be relevant to a kid living in a deli, struggling to survive.

"'There are occasions when applying too much critical thought and analysis to endeavors causes more harm than good, but it's always important to read all documents thoroughly.' *New York Post*."

Welfy whisks at cans of soup with a feather duster—not doing an impressive job of it, too tired to pretend effort. The night before, standing at the top of the stairs, he hadn't been quite ready to risk charging down to the basement to discover what would happen.

He had thought it kind of funny, as in funny-odd, that the entire time he'd been in Princess Nnnn's world, he'd urgently wanted to get back to Earth. Yet within minutes of again finding himself in Gramercy Deli, there he was, tempted by the very steps that might return him to that world. He kept picturing Nnnn and Raoul: how the princess maintained a protective watchfulness over her brother even while contending with a loss of morale or some logistical problem among her "people"; how Raoul always put himself between Nnnn and others, not allowing anyone but Prince Ffff to ever be as close to her. And then there were the Brundeedles in general . . .

Never been smiled at more in my life.

It almost made up for the Ceparids trying to kill him.

Almost.

He had contemplated the basement steps for close to an hour, and then—still with the Windex in hand—sat down on the stool behind the cash register, waiting for morning, not even attempting to sleep.

"'Improve your leadership skills by communicating in a way to which your followers can relate,'" Morton reads. "'Consider attending a course in public speaking. Your lucky numbers are thirty-four, six, ninety-one, forty-two, and seventy-one.' *USA Today.*"

Welfy managed to get Harlan out of the deli by 5:30 a.m., had really wanted him out by 5:00 in case Morton showed up earlier than usual, but Harlan isn't the easiest kid in the world to rouse from sleep. To coax him up and out, Welfy had gifted him a few day-old poppyseed bagels and a chunk of Philadelphia cream cheese.

"What's a Baloney King anyway?" he asks now, as Morton is about to read yet another horoscope.

Welfy didn't even know he was going to ask the question, but that's the thing about being this tired; a thought occurs to you and before you realize it, it's coming out of your mouth.

Morton glances up from his tablet computer. "Si Spielgut piqued your interest, did he?"

Welfy shrugs. "It's just that I don't know what a Baloney King *is*. Somebody who owns a warehouse full of baloney? Someone who has the best baloney? What?"

"It's not quality or quantity that matters, so much as how you employ what baloney you have."

As far as Welfy can figure, this explains exactly nothing, and so he's about to say never mind, forget he asked, but Morton leans back on his stool, folds his arms in front of him and narrows his eyes as if lulling himself into a trance of recall, as if the words he's about to speak come from a text memorized long ago.

"Si Spielgut was a small-time deli owner, much like yours truly," he begins, "and I suppose you'd call him an idealist, although he *did* impact, for the better, a great many lives on a practical level. Certainly, using only the most humble of luncheon meats, no one has done more to foster peace among diverse people than Si. Let no one tell you different, Welfy: Si Spielgut took baloney further than it had ever been taken before or has ever been taken since."

Welfy has serious doubts about anyone telling him anything about Si Spielgut, let alone anything *different*, such as questioning the extent to which the guy took baloney. But what, exactly, did *that* mean? How far can baloney be taken? And where—besides maybe on a picnic somewhere—does one take baloney *to*?

"It's important to understand," Morton continues, "that in Si's time—I'm referring to the early twentieth century—large segments of the American population were newly arrived immigrants who had suffered under strict caste systems or none-too-friendly regimes in their home countries. To these people, before they arrived here, America symbolized freedom from oppression. To them, America offered asylum from the past, a new beginning. They believed that in this country they would have the chance to be whoever, whatever, they wanted to be. But as you might imagine, Welfy, once these immigrants arrived, they found that life wasn't without hardships similar to those they had experienced in their home countries. At that point, because of Si Spielgut's efforts, nothing came to symbolize their dreams and aspirations, their freedom to actively pursue those dreams and aspirations, more than baloney."

"No way," Welfy says, which is his automatic response whenever Harlan tells him an unlikely story that he suspects by its very unlikeliness might be true. "No way. Get out of here," he says, not because he doesn't believe what he's hearing, but because it gives him time to absorb what he's hearing.

"You asked," Morton says. "Your choosing not to believe it won't make it any less true."

It sounded ludicrous. Except if Welfy hadn't been visited by the ghostly Baloney King, he might not have believed Si Spielgut the man ever even existed.

And the rest, I'd probably think it was all . . . baloney.

But how could he believe in Princess Nnnn and her world and not some deli guy trying to improve people's lives, to nurture the hopes and ambitions of the downtrodden, with meat? Welfy would likely believe a lot of things now that he would have dismissed as untrue only a day before.

"Okay," he says, "but what I'm asking is *how?*"

"You mean how did Si Spielgut see to it that baloney became a symbol of empathic largesse, a kind of all-for-one-and-one-for-all ethic in the five boroughs, but also the means by which peace was achieved between warring factions, and for many, the fulcrum of an accelerated, distinctly American upward mobility?"

"Uh, I dunno. I guess?"

"I take it you've heard of the Original Rays?"

"Heard of them, yeah. But—"

"What precisely have you heard?"

Welfy assumes it to be an urban legend: the existence of a gang whose hundreds of members are the tattooed men making pizzas in the Original Ray's restaurants that dot Manhattan like pepperoni. Men with gruff voices and accents neither Neapolitan nor Sicilian. Men with doughy bodies that suggest they eat too much of their own product. Welfy has visited more than a few Original Ray's pizza places, every one of which has been pretty ramshackle and time-scarred. Yet legend has it that these out-of-shape men in their rundown restaurants are a highly organized gang with advanced technology at their disposal, a voluntary security force that protects New Yorkers from being harassed by corporate bullies or from suffering under tyrannical labor practices.

"I can tell you that the Original Rays gang is no urban legend," Morton says when Welfy finishes relating all of this. "It exists. But what you don't know is that the Original Rays haven't always been a force for good and it was Si Spielgut who turned them. If Si had left no other legacy, his influence on the Original Rays would be enough to earn him a permanent place in history. The gang used to work as muscle for big business back when hordes of new immigrants—the vulnerables, as some described them—were housed in crumbling tenements and forced to work long hours in unventilated factories."

"Sweat shops," Welfy says.

"Yes. Except workers in a certain factory on Mott Street eventually had enough. They planned to rebel against those who kept them in inhumane living and working conditions. The factory owners, however, learned of the rebellion beforehand and sent in the Original Rays to quash it. Si Spielgut—until then an ordinary, local deli man—found out what was going on, and the night that the workers faced off against the Original Rays, he entered the factory armed with nothing more than a single baloney loaf. Forty minutes later, when Si walked out of the factory, all was peace. A greater understanding had been reached between the workers and the Original Rays. It was as if everyone had realized—a deep down kind of realized—that life was hard enough and they didn't need to make it harder by fighting one another. From that night on, the Original Rays allied with the oppressed and fought against the oppressors, and they've been doing it ever since."

"I don't get it," says Welfy. "What did baloney have to do with anything?"

"How Si specifically used his baloney is still a matter of debate," Morton admits. "Some assert that he used it to illustrate the benefits of mutual generosity and that, despite beliefs to the contrary, the material successes of one group did not negatively affect those of another. Others claim that Si simply gestured with his baloney while he lectured, in which case he must have been an excellent lecturer. All we know for sure is that for the next three years, wherever violent clashes were imminent, Si would appear with his baloney loaf, and by the time he left, all threat of violence would have passed."

"Why only three years?" Welfy asks.

"Something happened after that. Si closed his deli and disappeared for decades. No one heard anything of him until he passed away quietly, alone and scandalously forgotten, in a one-bedroom apartment in the Bedford-Stuyvesant section of Brooklyn. He left instructions to be buried in his deli apron."

Welfy isn't sure he's better off for having asked about the Baloney King. What has he learned that explains the deli man's visit in Princess Nnnn's world?

Spielgut said he wanted to tell me something, but—

"You mind bringing up some Bounty from the basement?" Morton asks. "We seem to be a little low."

Welfy turns to the shelf where the toilet paper, tissues, and paper towels are kept. The supply of Bounty is definitely low, but he doesn't move.

"There a problem?" Morton asks.

"Uh uh. Why would there be?"

Welfy positions himself at the top of the basement steps. He feels Morton watching him. He's still not sure he's ready to descend these steps.

I'll have to go to the basement at some point . . .

He lowers a tentative foot to the first step. Nothing. He eases down onto the next one. Still nothing.

"This is stupid," he whispers. "Just get it over with."

Like a gunfighter whose hand hovers above his holster at the start of a duel, Welfy holds a hand at the mouth of his apron pocket. He runs down the steps and—

He's just some kid in the basement of a New York City deli, with a hand at his apron pocket.

He carries a half-dozen Bounty back upstairs, where Morton is occupied with his red notebook, jotting down alleged wisdom from the day's horoscopes. Welfy shelves the Bounty, and with his feather duster brushes at various paper products . . . but there's something different about Morton . . . the deep worry lines in the forehead . . . the vertical creases in the cheeks, as if the tracks of former tears had left scars.

How could I not have noticed till now?

"I've been meaning to ask . . ." Morton says without looking up, " . . . my wife would like to have you over for dinner. How's tomorrow sound? It's Sunday and I can close early without hurting my bottom line too much. Let's say you come to the apartment at seven o'clock?"

It goes against Welfy's policy to not learn too much about the people he lives among at any given time, but—

"Sure," he says, because he thinks it curious that Morton happened to mention Si Spielgut mere hours before the man's ghost appeared in front of him.

And it leaves him winded, the surprising possibility hitting Welfy so hard it's as if someone has punched him in the stomach: Could Morton know about this Brundeedle-Ceparid business?

12¾

 DARK ROOM. TWO voices. One voice, male. The other, female.

"He's an orphan?" the female voice asks.

"Your question doesn't have a 'yes' or 'no' answer. He has lived as an orphan for as long as he can remember. He believes that both of his parents are deceased. So in a sense, yes, he is an orphan. Strictly speaking, however, he is not."

"You mean—?"

"A parent lives."

Somewhere beyond the darkened room: a car alarm, a siren.

"He doesn't know?" the female voice asks.

"He does not."

⌊**13**⌋

ARMED WITH A nug in a cavern full of deadly missiles, a Brundeedle has to be quick. A Nug is the most effective defensive weapon a Brundeedle can have, able to divert all incoming projectiles except Sticky Orbles into its snub-nose double barrels and reduce them to harmless particulates, which it disperses through a vent in the base of its handle. But midbattle, when hundreds of Rador-Blood spews are lancing the air, a Nug-bearing Brundeedle still best have extremely fast reflexes to keep from harm. A Brundeedle's Nug might be sucking in the Rador-Blood targeting him from his left flank when a spiked cube-grenade lobs in from his right and annihilates him.

Among the Brundeedles, Bloob and Prince Ffff have the fastest reflexes. Even as their population has been reduced to a modest number of subterranean nomads, even while warring with the Ceparids, between skirmishes and frequent relocations, Bloob and the prince have trained to keep their reflexes sharp.

As they're about to do.

Bloob has found an appropriate cavern for the training exercise, at a safe distance from the encampment. As always, Raoul and his friends want to watch. And sometimes, if there's a well-protected nook for the youngsters to tuck into, Prince Ffff lets them.

But not this time.

Because this time the prince intends to test himself to an extent he's never done before. There will be far greater chance of onlookers being injured. Only the well-shielded soldiers shooting at him and Bloob will be allowed in the training theater.

"You already know that I've never approved of these exercises," Grrrrmmph says, "but *fifteen* soldiers shooting at you? It's madness. Even if you are at your absolute best—"

"You shouldn't risk your life in *training*," Pogg agrees. "Not at this juncture in the war."

Princess Nnnn casts an imploring look at the prince. Her eyes tell him everything: that she's against the training exercise, that she worries enough for his safety in all battles against the Ceparids. Yet she knows better than to ask her husband not to train; there's no dissuading him once he's settled on a course of action.

Nnnn isn't the only one who understands Ffff's expression. No sooner does Raoul, at his sister's side, recognize its meaning than he shouts "Fcgxillm!"—*Bathroom!*—and runs away.

"It might not seem like the best plan *now*," Bloob says, "but this kind of training will ultimately help us defeat the Ceparids. Then you'll be glad we did it. I know *I* wouldn't have notched as many Ceparid kills as I have without it."

Ffff nods in agreement, but he's thinking about Welfy Deederhoth, not the Ceparids. He knows that he shouldn't care so much if Brundeedles want to believe an Earthling is their savior, not when the population's survival is at stake. What matters is that Brundeedles survive, regardless of how they manage it, or who helps. To be so bothered by the existence of Deederhoth is beneath a prince's dignity. And yet Ffff *is* bothered. And it bothers him that he's bothered.

He and Bloob wait outside the training theater while fifteen soldiers place themselves at vantage points along its perimeter. All of the soldiers wear ParaskinGuards on shins, thighs, forearms, upper arms, chests, and backs. But ParaskinGuards can absorb only one direct hit of Rador-Blood and offer no protection at all from cube-grenades. The soldiers must use the cavern's natural rock formations for cover. Armed with grenade launchers and Globulators, they wait. There will be no signal to fire. As soon as one of them sights the prince or Bloob, training begins.

Nug at the ready, Ffff steps cautiously into the cavern, just as he would on a mission into enemy territory.

From above left and right, jets of Rador-Blood target him. He swings the Nug to his left, and almost before the incoming gets sucked into its double barrels—shhhwhip!—he aims the Nug at the death-spew vectoring toward him on his right. He pushes onward, cube-grenades and Rador-Blood coming at him from every direction. Ffff can't neutralize all of the incoming missiles inside his Nug; there are too many. His progress across the cavern floor is fitful, uneven. He somersaults away from explosions, gymnastically avoids Rador-Blood spew. Survival seems unlikely, yet somehow—

He does it.

He reaches out and touches the far wall of the cavern. The missiles immediately cease. The fifteen soldiers emerge from their various positions, and Bloob, who'd been watching from the entrance, steps into the training theater. Ffff remains facing the wall.

"Prince," Bloob says, "that was the greatest performance I have ever—"

"WOO HOO!"

A celebratory Raoul emerges from a pile of boulders and runs toward the prince. The youngster shouldn't have been anywhere near the training theater, but instead of chastising him for disobedience, Ffff doesn't turn from the wall. Nor does he explain to anyone how, during the exercise, he had imagined that wherever he aimed his Nug, he was reducing Welfy Deederhoth to dust so as to never see him again.

⬡ **14** ⬡

SUNDAY NIGHT. DRESSED in his nicest clothes—dark blue Dockers and matching collared shirt he bought at a secondhand store, and his only pair of Adidas—Welfy rides the Lexington Avenue 6 train uptown. At 77th Street, he stares at a Continental Airlines advertisement on the upper wall of the car. *Your Commute to the World*, he reads over and over again, breathing deeply and evenly, trying to appear as indifferent as the other passengers.

Seventy-Seventh Street: just a single station in a long line of stations; not a reminder of unwelcome nights spent in cinder-dusted sleep beneath a concrete platform, hassled by scrabbling rats and onrushing trains.

Emerging at 96th and Lexington, Welfy cuts down to 95th, then walks east to a four-story brownstone between First and Second Avenues. The building's lobby door is unlocked and he starts up the stairs to the fourth floor. The hall carpet is worn to threads. Landings creak. Outside the door of apartment 4B, he hesitates.

Haven't been in anyone's home since . . . since . . .

He'd rather not think about it. What does it matter how long it's been? He feels like an intruder every time he steps into somebody's home.

Remember why I'm here. Find evidence. Prove Morton knows his deli's an intergalactic portal.

He raises a hand to knock on the door of 4B, but before his knuckles rap metal—

"Come in!" Morton calls from within the apartment,

exactly like a psychic in some horror movie, a man with a sixth sense who can feel the presence of invisible others.

Welfy half expects the door to open on its own and reveal his boss in a recliner across the room—as if the man can make things move just by thinking about them.

It doesn't happen.

He pushes open the door and enters the apartment, which is alive with shadows, furtive light.

"Welcome," Morton says. He gestures at the candles around the living room. "Sorry about all this, but the power's out."

The power's . . . ? Nothing's wrong with the lights in the hall.

"The electrical's screwy in these old buildings," Morton says, as if he can read Welfy's thoughts.

"You know when it'll come back on?"

"Not for hours, if the past is any clue," Morton answers.

Welfy figures now that he's here they might keep the front door propped open, to let in the hall light, but no—Morton shuts and locks it, and Welfy realizes that this is the first time he's ever seen his boss outside of Gramercy Deli. And it's strange: being somewhere with a guy he's only used to seeing at work. It makes Morton seem out of place in his own home.

Say something. Make small talk the way normal people do.

But Welfy's tongue feels heavy and useless. It's not as if he's a talkaholic at the deli anyway.

"How about something to drink?" Morton offers. "Cran-Grape? Coke?"

"Cran-Grape would be good."

"You got it."

A candle in hand, Morton retreats to the kitchen, giving Welfy an opportunity to note what he can of the apartment. Which isn't much. And not because of the unsteady light. The walls are big white blanks, empty of art or photos, and the furniture could belong to anybody. Simple and practical, it's the sort of furniture people order out of a catalog when they don't care what they have so long as they have somewhere to sit and eat. Except for the spiral-bound notebooks filling the built-in bookshelves, there's not a single item in the room to suggest that Morton or his wife have any personalities at all.

But so many notebooks: Morton has obviously been taking astrological notes for a *long* time.

"The Cran-Grape you ordered, sir."

Welfy spins around, practically knocks the glass to the carpet.

"Sorry," Morton smiles. "Didn't mean to sneak up on you. Elle will be out to say hello in a second. We ordered Chinese That all right with you?"

"Sure. Yeah."

Candlelight flits about, throwing into shadow the deli man's eyes and the hollows under his cheekbones while somehow dramatizing the creases in his forehead and the wide pores in his sandpaper chin. As he sets the table, Welfy understands what's different about his boss, what he was surprised to notice for the first time only yesterday: the guy looks significantly older than he did a week ago.

As if he's aging faster than regular humans.

"Ah, here she is," Morton says, in that same psychic way of his, because Elle doesn't come into the room until *after* he says it.

A mouth like a blossomed flower. A delicately curving chin. Elle is pretty—probably the prettiest woman Welfy has ever met, despite the black pouches under her eyes, which he's found to be common among people in the city, so many of whom look perpetually tired.

Elle's most striking feature, though, is her hair. Thick black hair drapes the back and sides of her head, skimming her shoulders, while in front the smooth black sheen is cut in bangs and covers her forehead so completely that Welfy can't even see her eyebrows. The hair above Elle's eyes seems as rigid as a helmet. A lot of hairspray must have been needed to keep it looking as it does, preventing the slightest tendency toward muss.

"It's good to meet you," Elle says.

Welfy nods politely. "Thanks for inviting me."

"Thank you for coming. I'm glad Morton finally got help at work. I've heard a lot about you. All good, of course."

Welfy doesn't know how to respond. He can't say he's heard a lot about Elle because he hasn't. And the candlelight is playing tricks on him. He hears Elle's words and glimpses movement of her lips, but her voice seems to be coming from somewhere else.

Despite the generic furniture, despite his resolve to treat this visit as a fact-finding mission, Welfy feels as if his insides are draining out his feet. It's the same sensation that he used to get when auditioning for placement in yet another family.

"Could I use the bathroom?" he asks.

"If you must," Morton jokes. "Just follow the candles. It's at the end of the hall."

Out of Morton and Elle's view, Welfy steps into the bedroom. Utter darkness reigns, a darkness more complete than what he'd experienced deep under the 77th Street subway platform.

Not sure what he's looking for, a hall candle in hand, he checks under the bed, inside closets and dresser drawers. He finds only an unsurprising miscellany of clothes and shoes. In the wavering light, he examines the framed photographs displayed atop the dresser: Morton and Elle at the Statue of Liberty; Morton and Elle at the Brooklyn Bridge; Morton and Elle at the bandshell in Central Park. In each photo, Elle's helmet-hair obscures her forehead.

Need to hurry. Taking too long.

Welfy's about to leave the room when he realizes: no digital clock anywhere. In fact, the entire time he's been in the apartment, he hasn't noticed a single gadget or appliance that plugs into an electrical socket. Not a TV or computer. Not even a table lamp. Nothing he can use to confirm that the apartment is without power. He flicks the light switch on the wall. The room remains dark.

So Morton was telling the truth?

Turns out: no. Because when Welfy stands on a chair to closely inspect the sconce—

The light bulbs are missing.

"Everything all right back there?" Morton calls.

"Yeah, coming!" Welfy hurries to the bathroom and flushes the toilet, returns to his hosts.

"Starting to think you'd fallen in," Morton says.

The food is on the table, all of it in plastic microwaveable containers provided by the restaurant. It's the kind of spread Welfy hasn't seen . . . ever. Sure, Gramercy Deli houses more food than this every day of the week, but that's supposed to be for customers. The array in front of him—Kung Pao chicken, orange beef, pork Hunan style, vegetable fried rice, Szechuan green beans, shrimp in garlic sauce, steamed dumplings, BBQ spare ribs, egg rolls—it's way too much for the three of them to eat.

Morton over-ordered on purpose. The food's for me.

Welfy mounds the stuff onto his plate, forklifting sweet and spicy goodness by the mouthful, relieved that Morton doesn't jokingly say, "No one's going to take it away from you," or anything like that, because he knows how he must look: desperate, greedy.

Slow down. Focus on why you're here, your mission.

He guesses that if he inspected the sconces in this room, he wouldn't find any light bulbs in them. And whatever Morton doesn't want him to see, Welfy's positive it involves Elle. When she lifts food to her mouth or engages in conversation, doesn't she lean away from the table so that her head is lost in shadow?

"I hope I don't upset you," Morton says, "but I have been thinking about something you once told me—that the people you ran away from weren't your family."

Welfy tenses. "Yeah? So?"

"I assumed either you were adopted or in foster care."

"Uh huh."

"Morton," Elle says, "he clearly doesn't want to talk about it."

"Whether they're adoptive parents or otherwise, they might be concerned for your welfare," Morton says. "Have you considered sending them an email to let them know you're okay? You could do it without revealing where you are."

Welfy feels a constriction in his chest, a fist squeezing his heart.

I've faced down Ceparids. I can easily handle needling questions from some old man, can't I?

But no way he's going to write any email. "I doubt they're 'concerned,'" he manages.

"I'm sorry for bringing all this up," Morton persists, "but since I've already put my foot in my mouth, I might as well see how far in it'll go. I want you to know, Welfy, that I have a few connections, customers from the deli who haven't stopped in lately; you haven't met them. Maybe I can help you locate your biological parents, is what I'm trying to say."

If he could, Welfy would curl up in self-protection like one of those roly-poly bugs he's always dusting off Gramercy Deli's shelves. He'd curl up and leave nothing of himself exposed to Morton, to the oncoming world, the unknown.

You think I didn't try to find them? he wants to yell. *You think I didn't annoy social workers for any information I could get? You think I would've stopped trying to find them if I hadn't finally been given a look at my file and saw that I could never contact them because—*

"They died in a car accident," he blurts, and immediately regrets it. It's none of anyone's business.

"I'm so sorry," Elle says.

Welfy stares at the nearest candle. Its flame blurs, and for a moment, he's glad of the uncertain light. He wills the tears away. His vision clears.

"Did you ever consider, Welfy, that your biological parents might have put you up for adoption because of *how much* they loved you rather than because they *didn't* love you?" Morton asks. "Due to certain circumstances of their lives—which, true or not, they felt were unavoidable—your biological parents might have believed that the only chance you had for a better life required them to give you up."

"Why do you care so much anyway?" Welfy wants to know.

Harlan probes into his business, he volunteers information; Morton probes, he wants to lash out and tell the guy to shut up.

But Harlan knows what it's like to be alone on the streets.

And Harlan doesn't try to help in the way adults do. Whenever adults try to help, regardless of how well-meaning they are, they usually just make things worse.

"Is there a reason I should *not* care?" Morton asks.

Welfy raises a hand to his face, his thumb touching the tip of his nose, his fingers wiggling. "Oooooeeebockbockbock!" he cries.

Morton, reaching for his water glass, turns statue; Elle too.

"Oooooeee!" Welfy cries again. "Bock! Bock! Bock!"

Morton and Elle stare in apparent confusion. Hand at his face, Welfy wiggles his fingers a final time, then grabs his fork and eats, no longer caring how greedy and desperate he looks. He packs dumplings and beef and shrimp and rice and chicken into his mouth as if to store it in his cheeks for the coming weeks.

Elle introduces lighter subjects—TV shows, movies, videos of silly cats. She and Morton pretend that Welfy's biological parents had never been mentioned, that his strange outburst hadn't happened. But Welfy knows nothing about any TV shows or cat videos, and he hasn't seen a movie in over a year. Reconnaissance mission or not, he wants to get out of the apartment. Awkward silences threaten, which Morton fills with talk of astrology, of constellations and tidal rhythms, till at last it's time to leave.

"Good luck," Elle says to Welfy at the door.

With what? he thinks, because her words are freighted with such emotion it's as if she's referring to something huge, some life-changing event that has to do with both of them. When she tries to hug him, he steps back abruptly and bumps into a closet door.

"We'll just shake then," she smiles, holding out her hand.

"Don't forget your leftovers," Morton says, giving Welfy a plastic grocery bag heavy with Chinese food. "Stay safe."

And despite not having learned what the guy knows about Gramercy Deli being the portal to Princess Nnnn's world, despite having no hard evidence to support the conclusion—

Welfy clomps down the stairs of the brownstone and pushes out to the street, certain that Morton does indeed know.

15

AT THE FREE computers in the public library, Harlan's read the horror stories—the articles detailing the way foster kids had been locked in storm shelters for weeks with nothing but pet food to eat, or beaten with mallets, broom handles, leather belts. He knows that more than a few foster parents take in kids just to collect money from the state, money that's supposed to be used to feed and clothe the kids but which the parents spend for their own good time, ignoring or abusing those they're supposed to be looking after.

Generally, Harlan avoids asking other homeless kids about their past, assuming that they will offer up personal info if they want to. When he questioned Welfy about his name, he hadn't expected to hear of group homes and Family Services files, and now, not for the first time, he wonders what finally provoked his friend to run away from the unmerry-go-round of foster care. Was it to avoid physical abuse? Or was it that, not having been adopted for whatever reason when he was younger, Welfy became practically un-adoptable, since prospective parents almost always choose a baby or toddler over a teenager? Maybe he just got tired of moving from family to family without ever feeling loved? Maybe he had gone out to play basketball at his local playground one afternoon, except when he got to the court, he just kept walking?

Even if none of Welfy's foster parents care enough to miss him, Harlan knows, there are others—ex-foster kids who, by running away, become the objects of exhaustive nationwide searches conducted by police, by organizations that advertise on milk cartons. *If you've seen Anthony Williamson, call 1-800-THE-LOST.* Sometimes, studying the faces of kids loved enough to make it onto milk cartons, Harlan can't help feeling jealous.

"Every now and then," he says, "I wouldn't have cared at all if things had been . . . different."

He and Welfy are sitting in the middle of Sheep Meadow—fifteen gently sloping acres in lower Central Park. These visits to the meadow after 10:00 p.m. have the solemnity of a ritual, although they don't happen with regularity. Neither Harlan nor Welfy has asked aloud what attracts them to this place at night, but Harlan suspects it has everything to do with the fact that, in these late hours, they have the entire meadow to themselves, a solitary expanse in America's most crowded city. With the park's relative quiet and the buildings of Central Park South rising picturesquely above the treetops, he and Welfy are able to distance themselves from the worry of their daily lives and feel the spin of the world, to be reminded of the open-endedness of things and arm themselves with a heightened sense of the possibilities awaiting them in the great Out There.

"I don't understand how it works," Welfy says.

"What?"

"The last time I went to the basement at Gramercy, when I had to get some paper towels, I made it down the steps and . . . ended up in the basement."

"Sounds spooky."

"I don't get why I wound up in a different universe or galaxy or whatever when I took those peas to the basement," Welfy says, "but not when I went down to get paper towels."

The blinking light of a helicopter passes high above,

against a background of clouds suffused with moonglow.

"For argument's sake," Harlan says, "let's pretend I believe you about the Brundeedles. I don't, Welf—want to make that clear—but let's pretend I do. You want to figure out why the basement steps sometimes beam you to another world and sometimes don't?"

"They don't exactly *beam* me."

"Transport you then. You want to know why sometimes you're transported and other times you aren't?"

"Yeah."

"I can't believe I'm suggesting this, but okay, let's examine the facts. One time you went down the steps carrying nothing. Another time you went down the steps carrying peas."

"So maybe the portal's only activated when I'm carrying peas," Welfy says.

"Exactly."

Welfy makes a mental note to try it, to descend Gramercy's basement steps with peas in hand, and Harlan drifts into another moody quiet.

Whenever low spirits overwhelm, Harlan tends to ask for a quiz. *Hey, Welf, why don't you randomly pick two numbers between 100 and 1,000 for me to multiply in my head? Again, please? And again?* It doesn't matter that Welfy won't know the answers to the multiplication problems he poses unless he figures them out first with pencil and paper. It doesn't matter because Harlan is never wrong. The importance of the quiz is that it keeps Harlan from stewing in negative thoughts.

"Want me to quiz you?" Welfy tries. "Naw."

Welfy's theory: whenever Harlan gets this sullen and silent, he's wallowing in gloomy remembrances. Used to be, Welfy thought he'd somehow have been better off with Harlan's history instead of his own. But to be given up as an infant by parents he had never known, too young to understand that they were rejecting him, was tons better than what Harlan had gone through—rejected when he was old enough to recognize what was happening, to feel the blunt-force trauma to the heart of a father dumping him roadside, hundreds of miles from home. *That* wasn't a history to wish on yourself.

"What happened to the girl who gave you socks?" Welfy asks.

"Huh?"

"The girl from the Hilton. What was her name? Sandra?"

"Yeah."

A light wind teases the trees to the south, their rustling leaves like the tittering of shy girls.

If Welfy wants to distract Harlan from brooding, he'll have to try harder.

"I came to this city because it's where I was supposedly born," he confesses. "Mt. Sinai Hospital. I came because I figured, how many Deederhoths can there be?"

Harlan stops picking at the grass, looks at him. "You're hoping to find out about your birth parents? You think maybe you'll write them a letter to ask if they'll meet with you, maybe even find out why they gave you away?"

"Uh uh. I can't ever meet them."

Welfy doesn't have to elaborate; Harlan nods, understanding.

"But I thought I might be able to learn about the kind of people they were," Welfy says. "I thought . . . I don't know, I might like that."

"And?"

"I haven't found anything out yet."

Because I still haven't tried, Welfy doesn't say. Because what if his research turns up nothing of value, not even the most basic facts of his parents' lives? For so long, he's lived with the possibility of getting closer to his biological mother and father through knowledge—of learning about himself by learning about them—that he won't know what to do if the possibility is gone. Maybe it was a mistake to have been tempted into self-knowledge by the name Deederhoth. At least then he wouldn't have run the risk of false hope.

He and Harlan could both use a distraction.

"The time I was in a future or alternate universe or whatever?" Welfy says, figuring he must have missed something in Morton's story about Si Spielgut and the Original Rays gang, some clue that explains why the Baloney King would visit him in Princess Nnnn's world. And Harlan, hearing the story of an extraordinary do-gooder deli man, might recognize that clue.

"Yeah?" Harlan says.

"There's something I still need to tell you . . ."

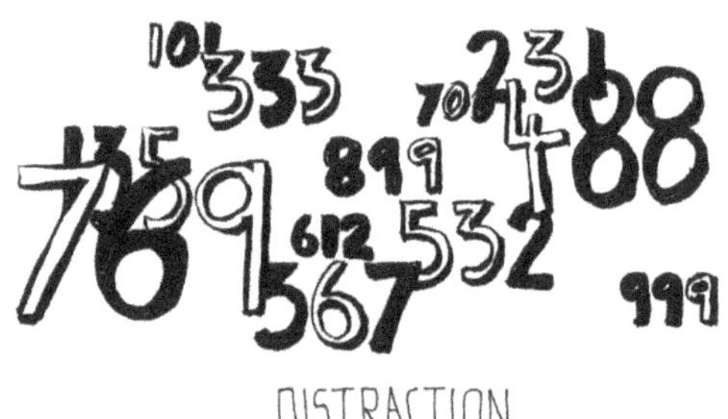

16

WHEN YOUR FATHER is an astrophysicist respected enough to regularly brief the United Nations Committee on the Peaceful Uses of Outer Space, you grow up believing that life exists on other planets.

For Sandra Zwerling, it isn't a matter of *if* contact will be made with alien life-forms, it's a matter of *when*.

"Why do you think that it hasn't happened already?" her father teases.

"Because you would've told me," Sandra says.

They have spent the morning at The Rose Center for Earth and Space on Manhattan's Upper West Side, where much of the information exhibited in The Hall of Planet Earth and The Hall of the Universe—how stars and galaxies evolve, how one can understand the Earth's history by study- ing cliff faces, mountains, and canyons—Sandra already knew. But never before had she time-traveled with her father as she did on The Cosmic Pathway, coursing back 15,000,000 years as the two of them walked the upward spiraling hall to the planetarium, where research astrophysicists from the Natural History Museum favored them with a private tour.

"Perhaps I couldn't tell you for reasons of global security," Sandra's father says now, on Broadway, holding the door for her as they enter the Dine-O-Mat.

It's unlike any restaurant Sandra has ever been to, with all available sandwiches, soups, salads, fruits, vegetables, and desserts in vending machines. Her father explains how it works: she feeds money into the machines and presses buttons C1 or F5 or whatever letter-combination corresponds with her dining selections.

"Once we've collected our meals, we'll meet back here," Mr. Zwerling says, giving her twenty dollars and throwing his jacket over a chair at a particular table.

While Sandra takes her time browsing the vending machine offerings, studying the keypads, Mr. Zwerling seems to know exactly what he wants and where to find it. If not for his constantly stopping to greet people, he'd be back at their table long before his daughter. Nor does his socializing stop once the two of them are seated and enjoying lunch. He repeatedly excuses himself to talk with diners.

"Who was that?" Sandra asks of a woman she had seen him hug.

"Oh, just someone from the NC15 nebula."

Sandra plays along. "She doesn't look like someone from the NC15 nebula. What about him? Who's he?"

She points to a busboy and the line of customers waiting for his help. The customers hold wadded-up clothes of some sort, which they surrender to the busboy when they get to the front of the line. The busboy puts the clothes in his gray plastic tub, the kind where dirty dishes are supposed to go, and then, with his hands in the tub, he takes on the concentration of a fellow at his workbench.

"He's from the next galaxy over," Mr. Zwerling says. "I don't give you the third degree about every acquaintance of yours, do I? That young man who was in such a hurry to leave our hotel room with a pair of my socks, and about whom you told me so little?"

Sandra's thoughts, as they frequently have, return to Harlan Mills. She has tried to find him. She visited the 77th

Street subway station and Zaro's bakery in Grand Central—places that she remembers Harlan mentioning the night they met.

Mr. Zwerling consults his watch. "Time to go." As on every previous afternoon since his arrival in New York, he'll be spending the latter part of the day with delegates at the U.N.

Sandra would like to take a roundabout way out of the Dine-O-Mat, to peek into the busboy's tub, but this requires cutting the line of people who wait for his services . . . whatever *those* might be. She'll have to peek into the busboy's tub next time she's here. Because she wants there to be a next time. Bussing her tray, she gets a good look at the contents of the garbage can: the sandwich crusts, the unfinished macaroni and cheese, Caesar salads, tuna wraps, and potato chips. The Dine-O-Mat on Broadway is a prime food source; Harlan should know about it. And she'll tell him. *If* she's ever again in his company, she thinks, not knowing that she would see him soon.

17

THE TRAVELER'S ALARM clock sounds at 5:15 a.m. and Welfy slaps it silent with a heavy hand. He lollops to the bathroom and washes up at the tiny sink. His elbows bang against the walls as he dries himself with scratchy paper towels. Dressed, apron donned, he switches on the deli lights and sets the coffee makers brewing, and by 5:50 a.m., when Morton arrives, Welfy's slicing onions and tomatoes, prepping for the sandwiches to be made later in the day.

"I come bearing the wisdom of the stars and bagels," Morton says, as always, though he's not the cyclone of energy he used to be—less a gust of middle-aged vitality than a faint breeze of old age. He distributes the fresh bagels he's brought with him into their appropriate bins. Onion, whole wheat, sesame seed, poppy seed, plain. "Leo the lion's got a thorn in his paw, so we can expect some cranky customers today," he says. "Elle really enjoyed meeting you, by the way."

"Yeah, me too," Welfy nods. "I liked meeting her too, I mean."

Morton doesn't mention the previous night again. Which is fine with Welfy, since he doesn't want to answer any follow-up questions about his birth parents—questions like how he knows they died in a car accident. He doesn't need Morton doing detective work of his own.

As if I can't be trusted to find out about my own family.

The day's business takes Welfy down to the basement a few times—both with Green Giant peas in hand and without—but at no point is he transported to Princess Nnnn's world. If there's one thing he's sure of, though, it's that he *will* again find himself in that alienscape beset by Brundeedle-Ceparid war. Because being transported to a future or alternate universe, if it happens at all to a kid, doesn't happen just once. That would be a cosmic rip-off.

Not that Welfy wants to further risk his life in other-worldly combat. But dinner at Morton's apartment had helped him realize something big . . .

The sensation he'd had of his insides draining out his feet, as if he were auditioning for yet another family who didn't want him—it was the opposite of what he'd experienced among the Brundeedles, whose smallest gestures toward him spoke of welcome, of relief in his existence.

Which he wants, needs, to feel at least one more time.

As soon as Morton leaves Gramercy for the night, looking more stooped and raisin-skinned than in the morning, Welfy goes to work: fever-eyed, knife in hand, so absorbed in what he's doing that he doesn't know how long he's been hearing Harlan's insistent knock at the front door.

"Lock it after you," he says, letting his friend into the deli and showing no sign of seeing the girl Harlan has brought with him.

That afternoon, Harlan had dialed Sandra's hotel room from a phone in the Hilton lobby. "Sorry about before," she said, and because he assumed she was referring to the close call with her dad the night they'd met, he didn't think he had to explain why he'd skipped out on her. Still, having asked her to come down to the lobby, he waited at a spot far from the elevators so he could easily bolt to the street if she brought her dad with her. But she showed up alone, and he was unable to believe how clean she looked in her clothes, as if she'd never been dirty in her life—totally unlike people who seem to have a layer of city grime embedded in their skin that no amount of bathing or showering can get rid of.

Locking Gramercy's front door behind him, Harlan motions for Sandra to follow Welfy to the back, where he's toiling over something propped on a stack of milk crates.

"Man," Harlan laughs, "for a sec it looked like you were sculpting a giant hunk of ham." His laughter chokes to silence when he realizes that Welfy *is* sculpting a giant hunk of ham. "Um . . . Welf?"

"Hold on."

Welfy pares off a curl of ham. A bus wheezes past out on the avenue. Welfy chips out a ham wedge. The clock above the cash register ticks.

Welfy steps back from his work, proud. "Take a look."

Harlan and Sandra maneuver to the "front" of the mis-shapen, knife-jabbed hunk of luncheon meat. Welfy isn't a very good sculptor.

"Poor defenseless meat," Harlan murmurs.

"This is Nnnn," Welfy says, "the princess I told you about."

Harlan takes a serious look at the ham, at Welfy, then again at the ham. "I'm sure I speak for everyone when I say, *That?*"

"Uh huh. The divots here . . . I'm not sure I captured the eyes. And her hair's real long, which I couldn't do with just one ham. I'd need another and would have to mush them together somehow."

"He's talking about the Brindeedle princess?" Sandra asks.

"*Brun*deedle," Welfy corrects, as if noticing Sandra for the first time. Then, to Harlan: "You told her?"

"I might've mentioned it," Harlan says. "Allow me to introduce you. Sandra, Welfy. Welfy, Sandra."

"Hi," Sandra waves.

"You told *her*?" Welfy asks again.

"What's the big deal? You never told me *not* to tell her."

"I didn't know I had to!"

Harlan eyes the scraps of discarded ham. "Hope you didn't waste any money on that meat just to carve it up."

"Nothing's going to waste," Welfy says, indicating the carefully laid wax paper beneath his work area.

Harlan pops a few ham shavings into his mouth, scoops up several handfuls and deposits them into numerous pockets. "So I was taking Sandra here around town," he says, "showing her the sights, you know? Showed her your old 77th Street haunt and the Holy Apostles Soup Kitchen, where we chose *not* to eat, thank you. She wanted me to see some place up on Broadway, but I was like, Who's the guide here? and offered to take her on a tour of the 42nd Street library. I had my own reasons for wanting to go there, which I'll get to in a minute, but she didn't seem very excited to visit a library—"

"I can go to one any time back home," Sandra says.

"So I tried to get her interested by reciting some basic facts that for a lot of tourists make this particular library a must-see destination." Harlan quotes a brochure he once read. "'The public library at 42nd Street is an impressive Beaux Arts building more than a century old. Its entrance is guarded by perhaps the most famous lion statues in the world, given the names Patience and Fortitude by Mayor Fiorello LaGuardia during the Great Depression. Every day, scholars and writers come from around the globe to utilize the library's wealth of research materials. These materials include everything from medieval manuscripts to baseball cards, ancient Japanese scrolls to comic books, much of it not yet digitized and available for download.'"

"But I still didn't want to go," Sandra says.

"No, you didn't. And that's why I had no choice, Welf, *except* to tell Sandra why *I* wanted to visit the library. And to do that I had to tell her the Baloney King story you entertained me with at the meadow. And telling her *that* meant I had to tell her about your Brundeedle acquaintances. I explained that I don't believe in Baloney Kings or Brundeedles, but that I had to go to the library to research this Baloney King I didn't believe in 'cause I was pretty sure the kind of info I was looking for . . . well, *if* the library had anything at all, it'd be in Special Collections and not on the web."

Sandra wags her cell phone. "It wasn't. We checked."

"Anyway, Welf, you can trust a girl like Sandra. Tell him what your dad does."

"He's an astrophysicist," Sandra says, "in town to give a talk at the U.N. on the peaceful uses of outer space."

"'Peaceful,'" Harlan elaborates, "as in not just how the countries of this planet might use outer space for peace instead of war with one another, but also as in, How about as a planet we don't launch anything into space that might send the wrong message to any highly evolved extraterrestrials passing by, be they Brundeedles or anything else? A girl with a dad like that, Welf—she isn't going to panic when she hears an unbelievable story about warring aliens, no matter how flipfloppy they are. Also, you should be happy people like Sandra's dad exist 'cause he makes your kooky imaginings seem less stressed-crazy and more scientific."

Welfy's not sure how he feels about all of this: it's a lot to take in and he never knows how much of what Harlan says is strictly true. "And your research?"

"What about it?" Harlan says. "Sandra and I are heading out for some pizza and I thought you might want to come.

My treat." Harlan unpockets a ball of crumpled bills—the remainder of the twenty dollars Welfy lent him.

Pizza?

Welfy's heart beats double-time. He no longer cares what Sandra knows. "You found something out about Si Spielgut, didn't you?" he says.

"To definitively answer that," Harlan answers, "requires a visit to one of this city's fine Original Ray's establishments."

The restaurant is typical of an Original Ray's—much-abused, in need of a paint job, every surface scuffed and dull. A single aisle leads to tables in the back, past the wide-mouthed ovens and the prep area where pizza dough is dusted with flour and kneaded into shape, past the service counter with cheese and pepperoni and sausage pies on display.

"So which one of you is Original Ray?" Harlan jokingly asks the two men behind the service counter. "Or are you both the original?"

The pizza men might be round in the belly, but they're no less intimidating for it. They scowl as if not above using annoying customers as pizza toppings.

"I'll have a couple slices and a Coke," Harlan says, cowed.

"Me too, please," says Welfy.

Sandra opts for a single pepperoni slice and an orange soda. One of the Original Rays is ringing up the order when Welfy notices a curious bulge under his apron.

Something tucked into the waistband of his pants.

The shape of the object makes a kind of imprint in the apron, and Welfy needs a few seconds to remember where he's seen it before.

A Globulator.

Not just any Globulator, but a semi-automatic.

"Something wrong?"

The question comes from the *other* Original Ray. Welfy didn't realize he'd been staring.

"N-No. Sorry," he says.

Carrying his food and drink, he follows Harlan and Sandra to a dining area whose furniture might have been salvaged from a restaurant that went out of business decades ago—wobbly plastic-topped tables, chipped metal chairs with red vinyl seats in various stages of coughing out foam.

"Right. So," Harlan says, seated, between bites of his pizza, "imagining myself in the Adidas of a person who believes in Baloney King ghosts, I figured it couldn't be a coincidence that Morton mentioned Si Spielgut to you, Welf, and then a little while later you had a visit from the man."

Welfy nods. "That's what I thought."

"Congratulations for agreeing with me. But if it wasn't a coincidence, then I concluded you probably couldn't rely just on what Morton said about Spielgut, because—"

"There might be something Morton's not telling you for reasons of his own but which wouldn't exactly hurt you to know," Sandra says.

"Makes sense," Welfy nods.

"As I realize," says Harlan. "Thank you."

It might be because Welfy has some idea, however vague, of what to look for—no, it might be because he knows to be on the lookout for *something*—that he's noticing some pretty odd stuff here at Original Ray's. Or stuff that would definitely qualify as odd if he could trust that he was actually seeing it.

Because that Globulator under Original Ray's apron? It's a homemade keychain—a column of wood with a bunch of keys attached at one end. Which Welfy knows because Original Ray comes into the dining area and uses one of the keys to unlock a door. And this leads to the second odd thing Welfy notices: the unlocked door opens into a little supply room. If this restaurant were Gramercy Deli, Welfy's sleeping alcove would be the supply room. And exactly where the deli's basement steps would be, Welfy notices, is another door.

"Anyway," Harlan says, raising his voice although he doesn't seem to notice Original Ray in the supply room, "I used the library's Lexis Nexis System to find out what I could about Si Spielgut. He was Baloney King from 1911 to 1914. He passed away in 1928, and I guess he was kind of a local folk hero, but besides his obituary, I found only a single article on him. It was in an old newspaper called *The Manhattanite*."

Harlan calls up the entire article from memory:

WHEN BALONEY ISN'T JUST BALONEY
BY DICKIE KRAUSS

Mr. Si Spielgut, owner of Spielgut's Delicatessen on Walker Street, has been on a one-man crusade. A crusade for tolerance among peoples. A crusade for a world free of persecution and oppression. A crusade for hope in the face of overwhelming odds and heartbreak. Of course, Mr. Spielgut is not alone in wanting these things. But what makes Mr. Spielgut's crusade different and – dare we say – more effective than the crusades of so many others?

In a word: baloney.

"All people are equal in their suffering," Mr. Spielgut recently explained to this reporter. "Suffering is the great leveller. I saw people who were hurting and wondered what I could do to help them. What I do best is work with meat, so I decided to help them with meat. Some people call it baloney, others bologna."

Questioned as to how, specifically, baloney or bologna helps Mr. Spielgut effect momentous change in conflicting peoples, the deli man answered cryptically: "Different circumstances require different actions. For example, when the Tryndian were fighting to avoid becoming a slave race, and every Nth Hour lazer-blizzards bombarded their cities, and even the rays were having trouble–"

This reporter had to interrupt. Who or what were the "Tryndian"? What was a "lazer-blizzard"? Or the "Nth Hour"? Hearing these questions, the Baloney King appeared as surprised as anyone might at such unfamiliar terms.

"Excuse me. I must apologize," said he at length. "Being a Baloney King while struggling to keep my delicatessen operating as a profitable business, I have not been getting enough sleep. I am so exhausted that I have confused actual life with a story I have been telling my youngest son every night before he goes to bed."

Apology accepted.

In future, perhaps we may better understand Mr. Spielgut's methods. Perhaps we will come to know how a common meat can, in part, have such an uncommonly positive influence upon countless lives. But until that day, let us take comfort in the fact that how the Baloney King succeeds in his crusade is less important, particularly in these trying times, than that he does succeed.

Mr. Spielgut serves as living reminder that a better world depends on the actions of each and every individual, and that we all have the means and power to help others overcome hardship.

This reporter, for one, hopes for Mr. Spielgut's continued success as Baloney King; may it ever lift our collective gaze to the nobler aspects of mankind.

Harlan leans back in his chair and clasps his hands behind his head, as if expecting thanks for having proved something important. But Welfy hasn't been listening too closely, because visible through the partially open door of the supply room, amid the five-gallon drums of tomato sauce and the nesting stainless steel bowls and the forty-pound sacks of flour—

Is that?

It is: a crate of cube-grenades.

And what are those?

A cache of what could possibly be long-barreled weapons, they are unlike anything he's ever seen on Earth.

Original Ray, having stopped to listen to Harlan recite the Spielgut article, now hurriedly picks up a drum of tomato sauce, locks the supply room, and returns to the front of the restaurant like a man with serious news to impart.

Unlike Original Ray, Welfy's response to the article is long in coming—so long that Harlan pitches his voice high and tinny and pretends to talk through a walkie-talkie:

"Chsssh. I think we've lost him. Repeat: I think we have lost Deederhoth."

"Huh?" Welfy says.

"Chsssh. Correction: contact re-established." In a normal voice, Harlan says, "You *were* listening, right? You *did* notice what was strange about that article?"

"Lasers hadn't been invented yet," Sandra whispers. "They weren't invented until decades later."

"Exactly. Which means they couldn't have been part of Spielgut's fantastical story to his son unless—"

"Unless he had access either to the future or to a world where lasers had already been invented," Sandra finishes.

"Correctamundo. And that mention of 'rays'? How much you want to bet that's a reference to you know who?" With a tilt of the head, Harlan indicates the supply room. "The article definitely got a reaction from *him*, didn't it?"

"You weren't keeping your voice down on purpose," Welfy realizes. "You *wanted* Original Ray to hear you."

"This is exciting," Sandra says. "I need more sugar. Who wants more sugar?"

Jumping out of her chair, Sandra carries their cups to the pizza counter for refills. The moment she's out of sight, Harlan pushes some folded papers across the table. "I also found out a little about the Deederhoths," he says.

Welfy stares at the papers, makes no move to pick them up.

"Sandra doesn't know," Harlan says. "I researched it while she was checking out some comics."

Welfy covers the folded papers with his hand and slides them into a pocket. Sandra returns with their drinks.

"Okay, so . . . you wanted Original Ray to hear you?"

Harlan leans over the table, motions conspiratorially for her and Welfy to *come closer*.

"If I believed in this kind of stuff," he whispers, "I'd say that the Baloney King article and Original Ray's reaction to it mean something's going on. Something big. And whatever it is, the Original Rays are involved, Morton at Gramercy Deli is involved, and it's been going on for a really long time."

Occupying a corner of the Original Ray's dining area is an antiquated arcade game called Alien Invasion, a first-person shooter, the kind that parents and teachers blame for teen violence, with players having to kill humanoid aliens in order to survive an all-out attack on an unnamed city.

"It's not like I haven't had doubts about pretty much

everything," Welfy admits, his hands expertly manipulating his onscreen avatar while Harlan and Sandra look on. He's trying to ignore the folded papers in his pocket, doesn't want to read them until he can be alone somewhere. Trying to ignore them, he lets his mouth talk. "The longer I've gone without returning to Princess Nnnn's world," he says, "the easier it's been to think I really *did* imagine everything—that Princess Nnnn and the others were just some kind of intense hallucination or whatever. It's why I was sculpting Nnnn's face, to keep her clear in my mind. But now that we know Spielgut visited other galaxies in 1911?"

"Wait. So you *want* to go back?" Sandra asks.

"Uh huh. I'm the kid from Earth in a dirty apron, right? I'm supposed to be The One Princess Nnnn's great-grandfather prophesied would save the Brundeedle race?"

"Welf," Harlan says, "don't take this the wrong way, but have you ever wondered why *you* are The One? I mean, what special talents or intelligence do you have that qualify you above all others to be the savior of a race?"

Welfy knows that the answer is probably none. Yet even after confessing so much, he still can't bring himself to admit that his reason for wanting to return to the alienscape has nothing to do with doubtful prophecies and everything to do with his feeling wanted, needed—even loved—when he's with the Brundeedles.

"I bet he has talents he doesn't know about," Sandra says.

Maybe it's the time he spent battling Ceparids, but Welfy's reflexes seem quicker. Playing Alien Invasion, he completes level after level of difficulty. Ten minutes pass. Twenty. Thirty. He's down to his last avatar, needing to complete yet another level to be awarded Bonus Life when—

A hand reaches in and jerks the machine's joystick hard

left, causing Welfy's onscreen avatar to misstep. The aliens take quick advantage: game over.

"What'd you do that for?"

Welfy swivels to see six teenagers gathered around, Harlan and Sandra having been forced several feet back from Alien Invasion. Dressed in white T-shirts and black jeans, Doc Martens and windbreakers, the teens all seem to be about eighteen or nineteen years old, the smallest among them at least four inches taller than Welfy and a whole lot bigger. They've arranged themselves so that he's cornered against the game console.

"Time to give somebody else a try," one of the bullies says. "You've been hogging the machine way too long."

Harlan's eyes are telling Welfy to say as little as possible. Welfy looks from Sandra to the bullies, then to the screen of Alien Invasion showing:

<blockquote>
High Scorers
  1. Ray
  2. Ray
  3. ____
  4. Ray
  5. Ray
</blockquote>

The cursor blinks, waiting for him to enter his name or initials as High Scorer #3. Why should he be afraid of six kids just because they're bigger than he is? He's fought Ceparids. He's survived Rador-Blood spew and Sticky Orbles.

And if I really am supposed to be The One . . .

He moves a hand to where his apron pocket should be. He isn't wearing his apron.

I'm going to get creamed.

"You deaf?" the bully says.

Welfy sees it in slow motion—the bully's arm extending toward him, shoving him. But slow motion somehow becomes fast forward—Sandra feisty and unafraid, clawing at the bullies and yelling for them to cut it out while they laugh at her and secure both Welfy and Harlan in headlocks.

"You six! Out of here! Now!"

It's the Original Rays, one of them holding a baseball bat, the other with a hand under his apron as if about to whip out the long, wooden keychain. Except now, again, Welfy sees that the keychain's imprint in the pizza man's apron resembles a Globulator.

"You're probably thinking six on two seem like pretty good odds," the Ray with the baseball bat says to the bullies, "and maybe you're right. Then again, maybe you're wrong. You don't know what my partner's got under his apron. Why don't you risk it and find out? Me personally, I'd like that. I'd really like that."

Years worry off Welfy's life before he and Harlan are released from their headlocks.

The bullies move leisurely toward the exit, as if leaving is their choice and they in no way fear two middle-aged men in flour-dusted aprons. The Original Rays follow them to the door, but not before the one with the Globulator/keychain under his apron turns to Welfy and winks.

"Well, well. Look who it is."

They're surrounded—Welfy, Harlan, and Sandra. Only a couple of blocks from Original Ray's, they made the mistake of turning off Third Avenue onto the less populous 26th Street.

"Let her go," Harlan says to the bullies. He motions at Welfy. "You've got the two of us. You don't need her."

"If she doesn't want to see her friends get pummeled, that's her loss," one of the bullies says.

Harlan nudges Sandra to go.

"I don't want to leave you," she says.

"Hurry up," the bully says. "I'm about to change my mind."

Sandra steps reluctantly into the clear. After a moment's hesitation, she races toward Third Avenue, her footsteps echoing between buildings and fading into the white noise of the city.

"Now we'll see how you do without your pizza-man daddies to protect you," the bully says.

Daddy.

Welfy's arm shoots out. He feels his fist connect with something both soft and hard, and before he understands that he's just punched his antagonist in the mouth, he and Harlan are running for all they're worth, the bullies chasing after them.

GAME OVER

(ALIEN INVASION, ARCADE VERSION)

⟨18⟩

THEY COME SPRINTING around the corner, their lungs burning, their arms and legs pumping, closer and closer to Gramercy Deli they run, Welfy with his keys out before getting to the door, working the key in the lock as quickly as he can, his hands shaking from adrenaline.

And then they're in—Welfy and Harlan inside the deli, but not before the bullies see where they've gone, which is what Welfy and Harlan were hoping *wouldn't* happen. Four of the bullies bang their fists on the door and front windows while the other two search at the curb for anything they can use to break the glass.

"If they get in here, we'll escape through the trap door in the basement," Harlan says. "We pop up onto the front sidewalk as they break in, and by the time they figure out what happened, we'll be gone."

Welfy has never known Morton to use the double steel flaps in the basement ceiling that open directly onto the sidewalk in front of Gramercy Deli. He has no idea if the steel flaps can open or if they're rusted shut.

"Sandra might've called 911," he says. "The cops could be on their way."

"But what if she didn't?" Harlan counters. "What if they don't get here in time? How would they even know to come *here*? And anyway, you want to explain who you are and what you're doing here to the cops?"

No, Welfy doesn't. But "if" the bullies get into the deli?

"When" they get in, Harlan should have said. Because they're definitely going to bust the front windows. Two of them are testing the heft of chunks of broken curb to heave through the glass.

Welfy grabs his apron from his cot, ties it on.

"You gonna make them a sandwich?" Harlan asks in disbelief. "I know you don't feel great about abandoning this place to these guys, but it's better than abandoning ourselves to them. The trap door's the best chance we've got."

More like it's the *only* chance—the bullies outside rearing back with their chunks of cement. Any second the windows will be shattered.

Welfy and Harlan stumble down the basement steps, Harlan missing the last couple altogether, his head knocking into the single, unshaded lightbulb that hangs on a wire from the ceiling. It's too dark to see the trap door.

"I can't find the stupid light," Welfy says, reaching for the swinging bulb, catching only air.

Flick!

A burst of white.

All around Welfy and Harlan, enormous jagged structures spear the night sky—buildings of some sort, armored with thousands of overlapping black plates and interconnected by tubulate passageways the color of darkly tinted windows.

"Holy squamosity," Harlan breathes. "You believe me now?" Welfy asks.

A spotlight sweeps over the surrounding terrain.

"You must be *really* stressed out if *I'm* here," Harlan says.

The spotlight pins them, its glare intense enough to blind. The ground at their feet erupts. Welfy feels the wet heat of Rador-Blood shooting past.

"Run!" he shouts.

Cube-grenades hail down. Welfy and Harlan maneuver through an obstacle course of explosions and incoming Rador-Blood. Leaping, ducking, scrambling toward no particular destination, scrambling in every direction, they somehow manage to avoid annihilation and sprint past a cylindrical monstrosity that's a city block long and four stories tall and resembles a jet engine. Hunkered down behind this piece of architecture: Prince Ffff, Princess Nnnn, Bloob, Pogg, and thirty-five Brundeedle soldiers, male and female, preparing to attack the Ceparid outpost known as EeEEecheE.

"What is that idiot doing?" Prince Ffff asks, making a face as if he's just swallowed a bug.

"Who's that with him?" Pogg wonders.

"He's drawing fire," Bloob says, bouncing up and down on his haunches. "We've got an opening."

Bloob jumps out into full view, does away with two Ceparids firing at Welfy and Harlan. The rest of the Brundeedles emerge from their hiding place and engage the enemy.

A sound like a thousand screaming gulls rends the air.

Ceparids appear at every vantage point—guard towers, balconies, windows, launch chutes, landing decks; Ceparids armed with sculptural Globulators, long-barreled Globulators, bazooka-like Globulators, and cannons that jettison Sticky Orbles.

The Ceparids unload a steady barrage of missiles at the Brundeedle infiltrators, requiring Princess Nnnn and Prince Ffff and the rest to protect themselves while simultaneously fending off those of the enemy closer to ground—the dive-bombing Ceparids with rocket packs strapped to their backs;

the Ceparids who prefer old-school hand-to-hand combat over the more technologically advanced variety, punching and kicking with the acrobatics of Earth ninjas.

Prince Ffff—Nug in one hand and Globulator in the other—fearlessly, accurately targets Ceparids while successfully taking out ninja Ceparids with punches and kicks and acrobatics of his own. He even subdues a Ceparid that flies too close with its rocket pack. Taking control of the rocket pack, he uses its previous owner's limp body as cover and zooms out over an enemy platoon, which he entirely annihilates with a cube-grenade.

Pogg makes steady progress through the fray, his combat skills not as awe-inducing as Ffff 's but still impressive. An efficient, practical soldier, Pogg rapidly calculates which of the enemy are likeliest to suffer direct hits and methodically blasts away at them without exposing himself to unnecessary dangers, always using what the landscape offers in the way of cover or camouflage.

A sculptural Globulator strapped around each wrist, Princess Nnnn proves as fierce and resourceful as ever. She tears through the fighting, and while she doesn't annihilate as many Ceparids as her prince, she puts an end to at least as many as Pogg.

And Bloob? He hoots and hollers and fights with his usual abandon—shooting at Ceparids with weapons held behind his back or between his legs, flipping and twirling, contorting his body to avoid incoming missiles. Bloob seems to be in many places at once—lending support to struggling Brundeedles while somehow also leading a charge against a newly exposed Ceparid contingent. His combat style is the exact opposite of Pogg's, which might fool us into thinking he's all flash and no substance. But the truth is, Bloob would be bored if he fought any other way. He fights like this because he can, because he's good enough to get away with it.

Advancing over the field of battle, the Brundeedles' desired destination becomes clear: a building shaped like an enormous, grounded pterodactyl, its wings stilled at a sixty-degree angle. A short distance from the Grounded Pterodactyl is a Ceparid waste facility, and Welfy and Harlan are trapped against it by a gang of Ceparids. It's a pretty stinky place to be—Ceparid waste doesn't smell like roses—but there's no time to complain.

"All right," Welfy says, remembering that he's wearing his deli apron, "if I want a weapon I'm gonna pull out a sausage, and vice versa, so maybe if I . . ." Welfy looks at the sky as if addressing some divine power. "I'd like a sausage right now! Yes indeed, I could totally use a sausage right about now!"

"This really the best time to be praying for sausages, you think?" Harlan asks.

Welfy reaches into his apron pocket and pulls out—

A sausage.

"Oh, no way! You've gotta be kidding!"

A wall of Sticky Orbles cannons toward Welfy and Harlan. It's only a matter of seconds before the prophesied one and his friend are goners.

Again shoving a hand into his apron pocket, Welfy comes up with what seems a fancy water gun—a lightweight, multicolored piece with buttons and levers galore. A small booklet is hanging from one of the levers.

"'Nebulizer: Instruction Manual,'" Welfy reads.

"Is there, by chance, a trigger on that thing?" Harlan asks.

Frantic, Welfy fiddles with every moveable part of the weapon. Smoke issues from its barrel and forms a cloud.

"Great. Fog." Harlan says sarcastically. "Been nice

knowing you." He squeezes his eyes shut, the Sticky Orbles only inches away when—

The "fog" intercepts and disintegrates them.

Staring in astonishment, Welfy elbows Harlan, who opens his eyes. They both watch, incredulous, as the fog drifts on, engulfing Ceparids and turning them into puddles of ooze.

The fog creates a buffer zone of momentary calm between the Earthlings and all of the fighting, then—

Shouts, an explosion: Princess Nnnn and the Brundeedles battling their way into the Grounded Pterodactyl.

"We can't just stand here," Welfy says. "C'mon!"

And he and Harlan run serpentine toward the Pterodactyl, ducking and dodging Rador-Blood, hoping against hope that they'll survive.

$$\boxed{19}$$

DESPERATE, THE FUTURE of their race at stake, the Brundeedles push their way into the Grounded Pterodactyl, which a reconnaissance NuNu had previously identified as housing a fleet of infinity-winged fighter craft.

"That was something!" Bloob enthuses, converging with Welfy and Harlan behind a pallet of what look like TV dinners.

Ceparid pilots and co-pilots, the last line of defense, guard the infinity-wings. Brundeedles train their weapons on the Grounded Pterodactyl's entrance, to prevent any of the enemy outside from entering. But Bloob doesn't seem to notice the surrounding mayhem, so nonchalant that he might as well be gabbing with friends at a barbecue.

"Drawing fire away from us like that—risky, you bet, but you saved a bunch of Brundeedles from being annihilated and where's the fun without the risk, right buddy?" Bloob spins, Rador-Bloods a Ceparid rushing toward them. "Ffff doubted you, but I knew what you were up to." He points his chin at Harlan. "This your friend? I'm Bloob. Swell to meet you." Bloob puts a thumb to the tip of his nose, wiggles his fingers. "Oooooeee! Bock bock bock!"

"Yeah," Harlan says, flinching as jets of Rador-Blood pass an arm's length away, "it's uh . . . swell to meet you too." Harlan touches a thumb to the tip of his nose, wiggles his fingers. "Oooooeee? Bock bock . . . bock?"

"You're *all right*," Bloob grins, and without taking his smiling eyes off Harlan, he aims his Globulator straight up and fires as a Ceparid careens kamikaze-style over the TV-dinner stockpile.

The floppy thing lands at Harlan's feet, won't be careening over any TV dinners in the future.

"Are we going for the spaceships?" Welfy asks, reacting to detonations and battle cries with no more than little glances in their direction.

"Ha!" Bloob laughs. "You're funny. You know perfectly well we're going for the 'spaceships.' And here I go. Yeeeah!"

Bloob sprints toward the infinity-winged fighters, his weapon spewing. To the left and right of him, Ceparids fall. Brundeedles strap themselves into cockpits, punching fighters' engines to maximum thrust, launching out into the dark sky.

"Take this," Welfy says, handing his Nebulizer to Harlan.

"Whoa, wait. What about you?"

Bobbing up and down as if it requires more effort to keep still than otherwise, Welfy says, "I'm good," then runs toward the infinity-wings, constantly pulling items from his apron pocket. Loaf of bread, cube-grenade, hunk of mortadella—whatever his apron supplies, Welfy throws it at the Ceparids. He bruises one of the enemy with a large onion, annihilates several others with a cube-grenade.

Harlan's not about to stand around waiting to be done in by a spray of deadly not-ketchup. Fog hissing from his Nebulizer, liquefying the Ceparids who give chase, he makes a beeline for the nearest spaceship.

Meanwhile, Prince Ffff takes on three Ceparids at once, distracting them long enough to allow a couple of Brundeedles to scrabble into an infinity-wing. He sights Welfy climbing into the very cockpit where Princess Nnnn is entering codes on touchscreens, preparing for launch. The cockpit hatch shuts and the fighter zooms out of the Grounded Pterodactyl.

His princess and Deederhoth have gone off together and there's not a thing he can do about it!

Annihilating his three antagonists with a cluster of cube-grenades, Ffff jumps into the cockpit of a nearby fighter, is closing the hatch when—

"Wait up, wait up!"

The prince looks as if someone's waving a stinky stick under his nose while Harlan clambers into the seat behind him. The cockpit hatch closes and Harlan barely has time to lock home a web of seat belts before Ffff accelerates to maximum thrust and they rocket into the sky, Harlan pinned to his seat, the skin of his face trying to puddle at the back of his skull.

Contrails shred the sky above EeEEecheE, where Ceparids and Brundeedles piloting infinity-wings battle, swooping and diving and twirling. Rador-Blood shoots from cockpit-mounted cannons: ships burst into giant fireballs.

"Oof!" Welfy says, slamming left as Princess Nnnn rolls their craft to avoid a pursuing enemy. "Ow!" Welfy says, slamming right as Princess Nnnn steers them hard to starboard.

Seat belts don't seem to be doing what they're supposed—

"Agh!"

Slammed left again, trying not to vomit from Nnnn's stomach-churning maneuvers, Welfy scans the control panel in front of him, wanting to help but unsure how.

"Activate the EeeiiiIIIkeIeIeI Annihilation Ray!" Nnnn shouts. "Activate the—"

The fighter veers hard left and—Oof!"—Welfy slams against the side of his seat.

Choosing at random, Welfy presses a green button on his

control panel. A brush lathered with shaving cream emerges, starts to lather his face. Another push of the green button and the shaving brush retracts into the control panel. Half his face covered in shaving cream, Welfy again scans the knobs and switches in front of him.

Annihilation Ray has to be one of them. "What's going on back there?" Nnnn shouts.

"Working on it!"

Welfy glances out the cockpit. Even if he gets the annihilation ray up and ready to fire, how will he know where to shoot? The infinity-winged fighters all look the same.

Can't tell which ones are piloted by Ceparids, which by Brundeedles, so how can I—

Nnnn abruptly kills the throttle. Welfy slams forward— "Agh!"—and instinctively extends an arm to brace himself. His hand hits the control panel as the pursuing infinity-wing flies past and a joystick rises from beneath Welfy's seat. A target screen appears in front of him, showing an X-ray image of the fighter craft. Its pilots are clearly Ceparids.

Welfy grabs hold of the joystick, aims, shoots.

The Annihilation Ray turns the Ceparid fighter into a raging cloud of fire and debris.

"Yes!" he celebrates. "Yes, yes, yes!"

"Prepare for YoYo Space," Princess Nnnn says, all business.

There is no preparation for YoYo Space. Welfy experiences a strange pull deep inside his gut and then weightlessness. It's as if his senses skip a beat—he sees and hears nothing—and when he returns to himself, he and Princess Nnnn are coursing through peaceful dark matter, safe from Ceparid threat.

For now.

I T'S NIGHT IN the Coringa region. But it's always night in the Coringa region: a hardscrabble moonscape, desolate save for the scattered ruins of past civilizations. Coringa's forever-darkness is a good thing, though, because if we saw the region by the light of day, we would drop to our knees and spend the rest of our short lives wailing in despair, so lifeless, so merciless would our surroundings appear.

Visitors to the Coringa region are rare. We find no sign of activity for miles in any direction until we pass a certain outcropping of black rock and come upon the Brundeedle encampment, where sleeping cocoons are being expanded and soldier-mechanics repair what damage they can on the hijacked infinity-wings.

Welfy and Harlan stand before a reluctant Prince Ffff.

"It's not that hard," Bloob says to the prince. "C'mon, you can do it."

"Yes, they have more than proven themselves," says Pogg.

Princess Nnnn takes her husband's hand and holds it out to Welfy as if manipulating a mannequin. Encouraged by the others, Welfy reaches for Ffff's hand, shakes.

"You both did . . . fine. Now I must see to something elsewhere," the prince mutters, marching away to be with his soldiers.

"He's really very sensitive once you get to know him," Bloob says. "Honest. I wouldn't worry about it more than a little bit."

Pogg grasps Welfy's hand and gives it a firm shake. "Tomorrow we will conquer. Or die."

"Very reassuring," Harlan says.

Pogg and Bloob go off to join the rest of the Brundeedles. Only Princess Nnnn remains with the Earthlings.

"I don't know how my great-grandfather knew about you, but he knew." She leans in to kiss Welfy's right cheek, but changes her mind and kisses him on the left instead.

"So . . . this is kinda different," Harlan observes after the princess leaves them.

Welfy watches Nnnn visit with the wounded.

"I want to ask a question," Harlan says, "just so one of us has actually stated it out loud. There's no way you could be making all this up, with me here, I mean?"

"I don't think so."

"If that ketchup or whatever it is hit us, we'd be dead?"

"That seems to be how it works."

"And you don't know how exactly we got here, or if we'll ever get back?"

"Not really."

Harlan surveys the Brundeedles. After a minute, he says, "I dunno, maybe I can get used to this. There are some cute girls here. I'll introduce myself around."

No sooner is Welfy alone than—"Ooooooooooooooooh! Oooooooooohh!"—Si Spielgut materializes next to him. Like his previous haunting, the Baloney King is dressed in a deli apron. The sole difference: instead of Gulden's mustard, he's holding a squeezable plastic container of Best Foods mayonnaise.

"I had a feeling you might show up," Welfy says. "What's the mayo for?"

Spielgut blinks at the Best Foods in his hand. "How'd that get there? *Why* is it there? These are worthwhile questions, I admit, as are all questions concerning condiments. But I think the more pressing question, Welfy Q. Deederhoth, is, what's on your face?"

"What're you talking about?"

Welfy lifts a hand to his right cheek. It comes away smeared with shaving cream.

The Ceparid fighter. The automatic shaver.

"Ceparids shave?" he says. "Why didn't anyone tell me I had shaving cream on my face?"

And in front of Princess Nnnn! I'm a total doofus!

As if urgently swatting away bees, Welfy wipes his cheek clean. "I don't even realize I've got shaving cream on my face and I'm supposed to be The One?" he mumbles.

"Yes."

Spielgut says it so matter-of-factly that Welfy's taken aback. He has sort of stopped worrying if he truly is The One, willing to tamp down his doubts and go along with the idea because he needs the Brundeedles' need of him. But Spielgut is so certain. How can the ghost be *that* certain?

"You want to give me some advice, that's why you're here?" Welfy asks.

"Correct," says Spielgut. "I wish to tell you that although you can lead a man to baloney . . . or no . . . when a baloney-eater learns to fish . . . ach, I don't remember. It will come to me if I try not to think about it."

The Baloney King hums, trying not to think about what he can't remember. If anyone other than Welfy can see him, they give no indication of it. Harlan is flirting with a quartet of Brundeedle females, and everyone else is in what might be called post-battle quiet—meditating on the fight they have just survived and on those yet to come.

"What happened to you?" Welfy asks, sure that Spielgut isn't going to remember the advice he wanted to impart.

"I got older and then I died. My memory isn't what it used to be."

"No, I mean . . . you did good things for people as the Baloney King. But no one knows why you stopped and it kind of seems like you just . . . quit."

Spielgut is suddenly agitated, apparently unaware that he's squeezing ghostly mayonnaise all over himself. "Deep breaths," he tells himself. "Deeeeeep breaths." His emotions under control, he says, "One man's baloney doesn't amount to a hill of beans in this crazy world, Welfy Q. Deederhoth. You ask what happened to me. I answer, the same thing that happened to thousands of people: World War I. Yes, I helped factory workers and others in need. Yes, I helped bring about mutual understanding and respect between employers and budding labor unions. But what did any of that matter when entire nations went to war, everyone trying to obliterate everyone else? My eldest son shipped off to fight in this so-called 'war to end all wars.' When he did not return, bitterness grew within me. I asked myself, what lasting good were my successes as Baloney King? Relations among a select number of people might briefly change for the better, but sooner or later these people would return to their hostile ways. The rich and powerful few would return to exploiting the less fortunate multitudes, believing that such exploitation was necessary if they themselves were to continue to flourish. The natural order of things, it seemed to me, was that people behaved like enemies, that everyone believed their own success could be measured only by their power over others."

"But people didn't always revert," Welfy points out. "The Original Rays gang didn't."

"No. They are the exception and have helped more people than I ever did. It took me a long time to recognize what would have been obvious to me had my judgment not been clouded by bitterness and mourning for my lost son—that without me, the Original Rays would not be what they are today. But even if I'd had no influence on those pizza men, I have come to realize that hanging up my Baloney King apron, quitting the fight, was a mistake. Even if my crusade did not have the impact I had hoped for, to do nothing is itself a kind of death. It is to give up on the possibility of a better world by letting the worst impulses of humankind have free rein. Life is nothing if not a struggle between our better and worse impulses."

This is serious stuff and for a minute Welfy almost forgets that the words are coming from a fattish ghost who's decorated himself with mayonnaise as if it were Silly String.

"I see a lot of myself in you, Welfy Q. Deederhoth," Spielgut says. "You are conflicted. You are uncertain but not unwilling. You are self-doubting while in the very act of doing what you doubt yourself capable of. You ask, How can I be The One? I answer, The why of things—or in this case, the how—is often not for us to know. You say, Maybe so. Maybe it is not unreasonable to expect answers, but since when have Brundeedle prophecies had anything to do with being reasonable? To that I have no response. It is a good question."

"That's supposed to help me?" Welfy says.

"In your world," the Baloney King continues, "you are an orphan. All of your life you have lived with families who did not adopt you. Do you understand, Welfy Q. Deederhoth? You have *never* been chosen. In your world, you are decidedly *not* 'the one.' There are forces in the multiverse responsible for where you are now—here, fighting alongside what's left of the Brundeedle population. I do not presume to name these forces, only to acknowledge that they exist. Whether you call such forces God or Allah or Melissa or Charles makes no difference. Why you specifically are in this position, Welfy Q. Deederhoth, I cannot say. But you *are* in this position, and *because* you are in this position, you have become The One."

The Baloney King is fading to invisibility when, in his most ghostly voice, he intones: "Use your head, Welfy."

And then vanishes.

BALONEY KING'S CROWN

$$\boxed{21}$$

O CREATE ART, some artists use oil- or water-based paints. Others use marble, wood, clay, tin, steel, fabric, audio, video, or a combination of these. In short, to create their art, artists use any and every material and technology available to them, whether the material be a product of the natural world or of human ingenuity.

Some artists even use pizza dough.

On Carmine Street in lower Manhattan: an Original Ray's restaurant that has existed for as long as anyone can remember. The place is so old that it might actually be the *original* Original Ray's—which is to say, the first such restaurant ever in business.

Most mornings, a certain woman comes to work at this Original Ray's, a pizza maker of such accomplishment that it isn't unusual for a crowd to gather on the sidewalk, watching through the restaurant's large front window as she performs her art. This pizza maker can spin a ball of dough on the tip of her index finger as one might spin a basketball. She can roll a wobbly disc of dough along the length of one arm, across her shoulders, and then all the way along the length of her other arm, catching it in her hand. She can throw dough-discs high in the air, juggling several at a time. But her feats aren't just for show; the woman makes excellent pizza. She learned her art from the pizza maker before her, who learned it from the pizza maker before him, who learned it from the pizza maker before him, and so on and so on.

This morning, it's still too early for anyone to have gathered on the sidewalk to watch the pizza maker work. She herself has only just arrived at Original Ray's. She ties on her apron and rubs a pinch of flour between her hands, preparing to make her first pie of the day when the chime above the door sounds and a woman enters. The pizza maker doesn't recognize the woman, whose hair appears to be glued to her skull, especially about the forehead. Yet somehow the pizza maker knows: the moment has come, the moment she's hoped for, prayed for, understanding all the while that its arrival was never guaranteed, prophecies not being as reliable as she wished.

"I've been sent by my husband," the woman says. And then, a question that would sound nonsensical to anyone else, but which the pizza maker recognizes as a code confirming that yes, the moment has indeed come:

"Tell me," the woman with the helmet-hair asks, "Does your baloney have a first name?"

22

"THE CEPARIDS STOPPED abiding by anything that might be described as 'rules of war.' The murder of innocent civilians, which we had at first mistaken for accident, we soon realized was *strategy*."

Pogg explains this to Welfy and Harlan as they sit around a campfire with the surviving Brundeedles. Along with the rest of his kind, Pogg is eating a yellow clay-like glop squeezed from a packet. He offers a nubbin of the stuff to Harlan.

"Would you like a taste of this?"

"No thanks," Harlan says, needing only a whiff to decide.

"We've been warring with those uglies since our earliest ancestors first bumped into them," Bloob says. "We have no idea why they changed their tactics after so long."

"Unfortunately," says Princess Nnnn, "these tactics have been very effective. By randomly targeting our civilian population, the Ceparids were able to destabilize not only communities, but eventually our civilization as a whole."

"My own family," Pogg volunteers, "my mother and father and older brother, were annihilated when a Sticky Orble exploded in Longish Beach, a residential quarter of our former capital city, Zalyx. It was the first civilian attack, the one we had supposed an accident. Had I been home at the time, I would not be with you now. You're sure that you don't want a bite of this fortifying substance?" Pogg again offers yellow glop to Harlan.

"Yeah, no. Thanks," Harlan says. "Welf?"

Welfy reaches into his apron pocket, comes up with a Globulator.

"Useful," Harlan acknowledges, "but not what I had in mind in the way of an esculent, which as any dictionary will inform you, is something edible."

Welfy lowers a hand into his apron pocket, finds himself holding an apple.

"Thank you." Harlan grabs the fruit. "And a little protein, if you please?"

Welfy dips into his apron pocket several times. Cube-grenades, sculptural Globulators, Nugs—he sets aside whatever weaponry emerges, and at length provides his friend with a meal's worth of chicken and turkey.

"Thththth," Princess Nnnn says.

Bloob digs an angry heel into the ground. A number of Brundeedles shift uneasily or simmer in melancholy quiet.

Harlan exchanges a look with Welfy. "Excuse us?"

"Thththth," the princess repeats. "It was an outdoor marketplace near the palace. My parents made a point of personally shopping there, to be among the populace. One morning, having hidden themselves under displays of Blech Berries and Grody Grains, a company of Ceparids attacked the shoppers, slaughtering hundreds. Both my mother and father lost their lives at Thththth."

"Mine too," says Bloob.

"And mine," says another Brundeedle.

Others mention siblings, grandparents, aunts and uncles lost at the marketplace massacre.

"The rest of my family," Princess Nnnn goes on, "except for my brother Raoul, were among the casualties in the Battle for Zalyx."

Brundeedles who hadn't lost relatives at Thththth or the Battle for Zalyx had lost them elsewhere, at other times: when Ceparids had rigged a hover-sled loaded with cube-grenades to explode at a busy intersection; in a commuter corridor, when Sticky Orbles had turned rush hour into lifeless desolation; at popular entertainment venues, during some show or other, when heavily-armed Ceparids suddenly appeared and annihilated entire audiences. Public parks, places of business and worship—nowhere had been safe.

"The thing I don't understand," Welfy says, "is how Grrrrmmph—"

"Gesundheit," Harlan says.

"No, Grrrrmmph is the older guy I told you about. But I don't understand why he's the *only* older Brundeedle I've ever seen."

For a time, no one speaks. Then, staring into the fire, Prince Ffff says, "To be a member of the military, Brundeedles once had to reach a certain age. But between regular battles with Ceparids and their random attacks on civilians, our soldier ranks thinned and there weren't enough Brundeedles of proper age to fill them. It became necessary to lower the age requirement for military recruits. Over time the ranks again thinned, civilians eligible to join were too few, and the age requirement for recruits was again lowered. This happened repeatedly until our population consisted wholly of the elderly and the young. The elderly did not fare well after we'd been forced underground by Ceparid aggression. We are now all that remain."

Brundeedles: a race of orphans, an orphaned race.

"I've lost family too," Welfy hears himself say. "My parents were killed before I was old enough to remember them, and

I've spent my entire life either with people who pretended I was their kid or else in group homes for kids nobody wants."

It feels important to reciprocate somehow, to offer up part of himself as Pogg and Princess Nnnn and others have offered of themselves. It feels necessary—here, now: the intimacy of shared stories.

"George and Eileen Henning, my last foster parents?" Welfy says. "For the ten months, three days, and six hours I lived with them, a meal was never a sure thing. Not for me. They kept their pantry and kitchen cabinets locked. Refrigerator and freezer too. On top of what George Henning made as a traffic cop, he and his wife got money from the state for taking me into their house, but they also kept my quota— that's the money I was supposed to get to spend on myself like an allowance. So while the Hennings had money for food and always ate plenty, I couldn't even *buy* food most of the time. I took jobs whenever I could—just a day's work usually, like raking leaves in somebody's front yard or something, never enough to earn me more than a couple of meals."

Welfy's voice rises and falls: anger, as if the events he describes are happening all over again, alternating with resigned bitterness toward his past. He can't unremember his time with the Hennings, no matter how hard he wishes there was nothing to unremember.

"Every night at dinner," he says, "I had to sit in this hard-backed wooden chair. My feet had to be close together on the floor and my hands flat on my thighs, and I had to sit like that and watch the Hennings eat. If I didn't sit like that, I'd get no dinner. If I did sit like that, I *might* get nothing, but at least there was a chance of food. Except even if I was given something to eat, it'd be stuff like crackers and peanut butter, which just reminded me how hungry I really was.

Leftovers were always locked in the fridge; I never got them. I kept expecting social workers to show up and tell me the placement wasn't working out and I'd no longer be living with the Hennings, because that's what'd happened with every placement up till then. So when no social worker ever showed up, I complained to Family Services that I was being starved. Complaining only made things worse. Nobody from Family Services checked to see if the kitchen was all locked up, like I said. The Hennings denied everything, then got even more stingy when it came to feeding me. I was scrounging for food in garbage cans and wherever on a regular basis and figured things couldn't get much worse if I ran away. I was done forever with Family Services and group homes. One night I overheard the Hennings talking about adopting me permanently, and *that* made running away seem like my best option. So it's what I did."

For some reason, Welfy can't bring himself to look in Harlan's direction. How much the Brundeedles comprehend of what he's said, he has no idea.

All those hours with social workers and shrinks who tried to get me to talk about myself and not until I'm at a campfire with a bunch of aliens . . .

"It's an excellent thing you ran away when you did, Welf," Harlan says, "'cause if you hadn't, the people of Earth would be in a bad way—particularly in the New York metropolitan area. Everyone here knows that Welfy works in a deli, right? But I bet he's been too modest to tell you exactly what it *means* to work in a deli. I bet he said that he can't possibly be your prophesied savior 'cause it's just not the kind of thing he's cut out for. But on Earth, that's exactly what Welfy is—a savior." Harlan eases an arm around the female at his side. "A deli is one of the most important institutions we have on Earth.

Lots of hugely valuable goods are kept in delis, and a kid has to be pretty special to work in one: millions want to, few are chosen. A deli kid has to protect the deli's valuable goods from people so nasty they make the Ceparids seem nice, and he does this so that he can provide the valuable goods to desperate customers. Take last week, for example. These guys wearing ankle-length coats forced their way into Gramercy, where Welf works. Every customer in the place ran out 'cause it didn't take a genius to see the guys meant trouble: they had huge swords—cutlasses—under their coats. So Welfy's making chicken salad behind the counter when these guys show up with their cutlasses, right? Chicken salad is a rare commodity where we come from and Welf figured it's what the guys wanted—chicken salad. But no. The most menacing cutlass-wielder, the one whose scowl hurt your eyes just to look at, he points his weapon at Welfy and says, 'Gimme all your cheese.' I should mention that where we come from cheese is rarer and more valuable than chicken salad. 'Gimme all your cheese!' the lowlife says. But does Welfy panic? He doesn't. Slowly, very slowly, he takes a block of American cheese from the deli case and holds it out to the lowlife. Like he's surrendering it, you know? The lowlife reaches for it, and then—bam! Welfy bashes him with the cheese. For a long minute you can't see what's happening 'cause cutlasses and bodies are swinging every which way, but when things settle, there's Welfy, cutlasses in each hand, standing over the lowlifes who tried to steal his cheese but are now piled in the middle of the deli. And what does Welfy do then? He steps calmly back behind the counter, sets down the cutlasses, and finishes making chicken salad to feed his desperately needy customers."

The Brundeedles turn awed faces to Welfy—all except Prince Ffff, who glumly pokes the fire with a stick. Welfy smiles uneasily at his lap, shrugs, as if to say, *My friend's story? It's nothing.*

"Deli kids have to face dangers ten times worse than that every minute of every hour of every day," Harlan concludes. "And Welf's the best of them."

"I knew it was an honor to have you fighting with us," Bloob says to Welfy, "but not *this* much of an honor."

"Yes," Pogg says. "However, even with his help, we'll need our rest. Good night."

Others bid good night and retire with Pogg into the darkness beyond the fire's dwindling glow. Thirty-odd Brundeedles become twenty, ten.

"Allow me to accompany you to your sleep cocoon," Harlan says to the female at his side.

Only Prince Ffff, Princess Nnnn, and Welfy remain by the fire.

"Your friend cares a lot about you," the princess says.

Welfy turns to her. "Yeah? How can you tell?"

"It's obvious in the way he speaks of you."

Welfy's never thought about it before, even though he and Harlan have tag-teamed the hardships of New York City streets: how much they might care for each other.

"Folgamo," Ffff remarks.

The prince stands, waits for Nnnn to rise and join him. She doesn't, and he huffs off into the dark.

"My father had arranged for me to marry someone else," Nnnn says, staring after her husband. "It was the custom that a young princess marry a man of her father's choosing. I didn't understand and thought blind adherence to tradition foolish.

I had fallen in love with an arrogant young soldier and I married him after my father was annihilated at Thththth." The princess places a gentle hand on Welfy's forearm. "Please, don't be offended by Ffff's lack of belief in the prophecy."

"I kind of don't blame him," Welfy says, keeping his arm perfectly still. His entire body feels concentrated on the spot where Nnnn is touching him.

"Ffff has such anger over what's become of our race that he would like the impossible—to annihilate the Ceparids by himself. He won't admit it, but I believe he worries that you compromise his ability to lead, that being The One, others might consider you their leader."

The fire pops and smokes, dying. Princess Nnnn's touch is gone: her hand in her own lap.

"On your planet, do you have a girlfriend?" she asks.

"Uh uh."

"Your work at the deli is too dangerous perhaps?"

"Yeah, that's it," Welfy snorts. He can't remember the last time he voiced anything even close to a laugh. "You think we really have a chance against the Ceparids? I mean, I know you *have* to believe there's a chance, otherwise . . . no, never mind. Waiting for tomorrow gives me too much time to think. Forget I tried to speak."

"You want to know if I believe we will defeat the Ceparids," Princess Nnnn says, on her feet, about to go in search of her husband. "I believe now more than ever. As do many others. Because of you. You give us faith."

Alone, Welfy reaches into his pocket to retrieve the folded papers Harlan gave him at Original Ray's—alleged evidence of the Deederhoth family. With tomorrow's battle against the Ceparids, he might not have another chance to read them.

One of the papers is a printout of a twelve-year-old news item from the *New York Post*. It describes a taxi that jumped the sidewalk at First Avenue and 68th Street and crashed into an Original Ray's pizza joint, killing Mr. and Mrs. Melvin Deederhoth as well as several others.

The second paper is a printout from the *New York Times*:

OBITUARY

Mr. and Mrs. Melvin Deederhoth died July 11 in New York City. Successful restaurateurs, the couple volunteered much of their time to Louise Wise Services, a local adoption agency, as well as to various charitable organizations that serve underprivileged children. They leave no survivors.

Welfy's vision goes wonky and he makes no attempt to stop his tears from falling. The last of the fire's embers firefly off into the night, the sky speckled with light from stars dead long ago.

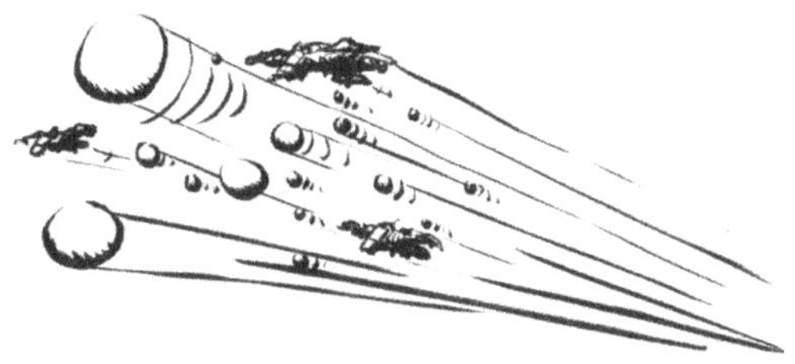

CEPARID METROPOLIS

23

DEEP IN THE Coringa region sits the most important Ceparid metropolis in the galaxy. Except for the ruins of the past civilization that once occupied the site and the fact that it's a whole lot bigger and more expansive, it looks much the same as the Ceparid military outpost known as EeEEecheE, having the same huge reptilian structures connected by tubular walkways. It's a bustling place, this Ceparid metropolis, with denizens dining in restaurants, drinking in bars, zipping around on hover-scooters and on plasma-powered jet boards that resemble the skateboards of Earth.

Were we able to stroll through this Ceparid city without being targeted for annihilation, we might find ourselves walking down a wide avenue toward what was once a great palace. Entering this palace, we would pass through a foyer to a large room with a vaulted ceiling, its walls decorated with elaborate, stone tile work and its chandeliers thick with dust. On the floor, we would see a splotchy goo trail leading to the far end of the dusky room, to an enormous, fleshy creature covered in a thin membrane of goo.

The Ceparid queen: Craetella.

The queen would be jiggling slightly, producing a constant squishing sound. At ground level on her slug-like body: a kind of loose-lipped mouth. Slathered with goo, Ceparids would spill from this squishing orifice onto the floor.

We would have witnessed Craetella giving birth to her newest soldiers.

MARMADILLION

24

THE MORNING FIRE has been suffocated with dirt, the sleeping cocoons packed, the hijacked infinity-wings repaired and readied for flight.

"Xoi jlicgalm ah ilmraimol," says Grrrrmmph, giving the Brundeedles a pep talk via vidcast. "Am gxo jcml lr gxo Tryndian. Gxo rlimoi Tryndian kcjcio."

"Homing NuNu reached Craetella's nest," Bloob translates for Welfy and Harlan. "In the old Tryndian palace. Tryndians were the first population annihilated by the Ceparids. Not the brightest species in the universe, but doesn't mean they deserved extinction, am I right?"

Grrrrmmph lifts his arms in a gesture of victory, his voice booming. "Jog fh kfg cm oml gl gxo gbicmmb lr Craetella!"

The Brundeedles cheer, priming themselves for battle.

"Don't leave without me," Harlan whispers to Welfy.

Walking to the outskirts of camp, Harlan snags a roll of toilet paper from a stash of Brundeedle necessities—glad to find that toilet paper is toilet paper even in this world. Behind dried-out brush, he pulls down his pants and squats. Grrrrmmph's voice, punctuated by Brundeedle cheers, reaches him from the near-distance. He waits for his body to do its business. A furry creature the size of a squirrel scurries around the foliage and looks at him.

"Hey there, little fella," Harlan says. "You're a cute thing, aren't you?"

The creature cocks its head and blinks.

"If I ever get back to Earth, you want to come with me? You could be the pet of this girl Sandra I know. Hey, you okay, little guy?"

The creature seems to be choking, struggling to cough up a furball. It gulps air, its body convulsing.

"Wasn't expecting *that*," Harlan says, because the creature seems to be convulsing on purpose—as a method of puffing itself up, expanding.

It's strange that the creature can get bigger at all, but even stranger and scarier is that it's enlarging to a size Harlan would not, even in this far-out land, have imagined possible. The creature takes on the proportions of an impossibly muscled adult man, with claws and teeth and a hide of dagger-sharp quills.

And it's *still growing*.

Scrambling to pull up his pants, Harlan makes it around the stand of brush before the beast opens its mouth and flicks out its long tongue, missing him by just milliglips—which is to say, only barely.

"Huge, hideous beastie!" Harlan yells, tripping toward the gathered Brundeedles. "Huge, hideous beastie!"

Everyone, including the vidcast image of Grrrrmmph, turns to him. The beast stomps into full view.

"Marmadillion!" someone shouts, and suddenly, as if by some secret marmadillion signal, small versions of the creatures pop out of holes in the ground throughout camp. All of them gulp air, puffing themselves up, growing bigger and bigger and bigger.

Zip! The vidcast of Grrrrmmph dematerializes.

Tongues flicking every which way, the marmadillions attack.

Brundeedles scramble toward the infinity-wing fighters,

unholstering weapons and blasting at the beasts. But Rador-Blood has little effect: just leaves red splatters on the marmadillions' thick hides, making them look as if they've been shot with paint balls. Cube-grenade explosions momentarily disorient them, singe their fur, but nothing more.

"Different molecular makeup or something!" Bloob calls out, seeing Welfy's questioning look. "We can't annihilate them!"

As always in a skirmish, Bloob frequently risks his own life, jumping between Brundeedles and attacking marmadillions. Like Ffff, who annoys the beasts with Rador-Blood so that soldiers can make it to their infinity-wings and escape, he provides cover.

But it's impossible to save everyone.

Marmadillions tear off Brundeedle arms and legs, chomp on them as if they're so much beef jerky. One particularly enormous marmadillion seems determined to make a snack of Welfy and Harlan, cutting them off from their only means of escape—the infinity-wing fighters.

Welfy reaches into his apron pocket, pulls out—

A chunk of headcheese.

"Not what I . . ."

He throws the headcheese aside and again digs into his apron pocket, not noticing that the marmadillion lunges after it, beating it up, devouring it, leaving a clear path to the fighters.

"Got an opening!" Harlan yells, quick-footing it to the infinity-wings.

Welfy dashes after his friend, about to scrabble into the ship Nnnn is prepping for launch when Prince Ffff stops him.

"No. You go with . . ." The prince points at Harlan, who's climbing into a nearby fighter.

"Ha ha," Welfy says, "that's funny. I'll get killed."

Prince Ffff remains stone-faced.

Welfy tries again. "No, see, we're both gunners so—"

"Xo ilmoh dagx mo," Princess Nnnn says, looking sternly at her husband.

Ffff turns to her, frowning. "Icmg xo kajlg xah ldm iicrg? Ah gxcg hl dilmu?"

No way Welfy is going to stay in the open while the royal couple argue. He climbs into the cockpit with Princess Nnnn.

"Xo ilmoh dagx mo!" the princess says to her husband in the firmest voice Welfy has ever heard her use.

She closes the cockpit hatch. Prince Ffff stands a moment amid the carnage, glaring at Welfy. He jumps into the infinity-wing where Harlan's already taken a seat, punches the maximum thrust button and is gone, jettisoned into space by the fighter's powerful engine. His is one of the last infinity-wings to zoom off, leaving a dozen Brundeedles dead on the ground as main course for the marmadillions' bloody feast.

"Hey, uh . . . thanks," Welfy says, strapped into the fighter's gunner seat as Princess Nnnn pilots them through space. "For, you know . . ." he moves his hands up and down as if they're two sides of an unevenly tipped scale, " . . . me, your husband, me."

"You are The One. The prophecy must be fulfilled," Princess Nnnn says.

"The prophecy. Yeah. Duh."

Welfy is seated directly behind the princess. She can't see him, but he still tries to hide his disappointment. Because hadn't he sort of thought that maybe, just maybe . . . well, Ffff aside, hadn't he kind of hoped that she *liked* him liked him?

He's staring out the starboard window when—

A burst of flame. And another.

Exploding asteroids.

Asteroids don't usually explode without reason and these are no exception. They are being destroyed by the infinity-wing trailing Welfy and Princess Nnnn, the one carrying Prince Ffff and Harlan, in which—

"Jeez, what were those things?" Harlan asks, referring to the marmadillions.

Prince Ffff doesn't answer. He punches a button on his steering apparatus and sends bursts of Rador-Blood at asteroids on either side of Welfy's infinity-wing. "No, he doesn't want to sniggle her, nooo," he broods, firing another round of Rador-Blood and blowing up another asteroid. "Big, important Earthling in his apron come to rescue the desperate Brundeedle customers." He fires yet another round of Rador-Blood; an asteroid explodes into shards. "He couldn't rescue himself from a grumpy koalabala!"

Harlan tucks himself deeper into his seat and thinks better of asking this freakazoid any more questions.

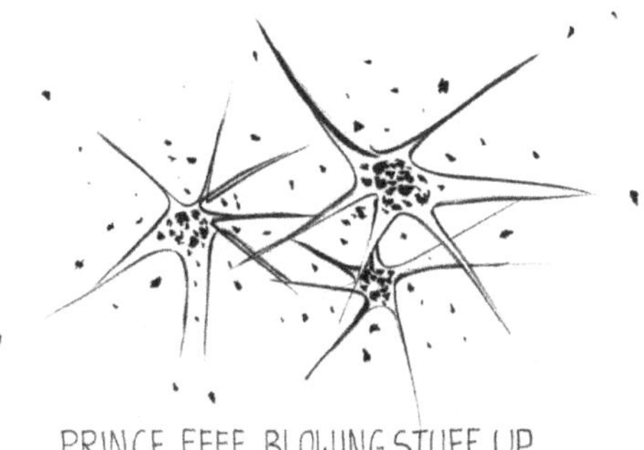

PRINCE FFFF BLOWING STUFF UP

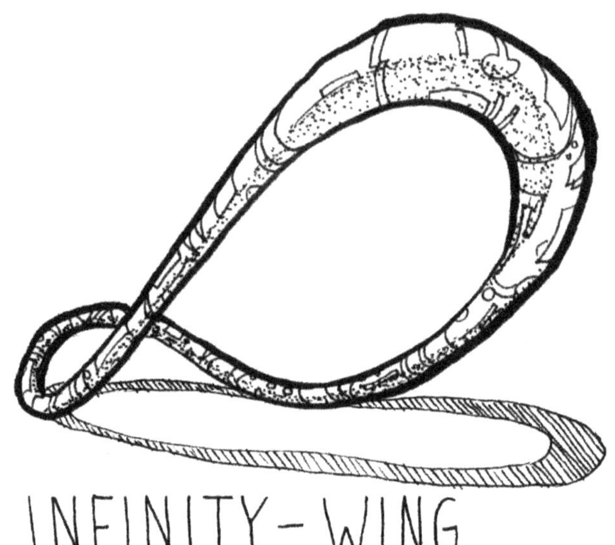

INFINITY-WING

25

THE INFINITY-WINGS ARE abandoned, Craetella's stronghold—the Ceparid metropolis built on the ruins of the old Tryndian city—visible in the near distance.

"Stay low and close together," Prince Ffff urges. Without waiting, he trots into the darkness.

Princess Nnnn, Bloob, Pogg and the rest of the Brundeedles follow, moving swift and silent in battle crouches.

"Next time," Harlan says to Welfy, "try being the prophesied hero in a beachfront paradise, will you? Someplace with sunny, mild weather, where we'll always have comfortable shelter, clean clothes, and plenty of well-prepared food."

"I'll see what I can do," Welfy smiles. But right now, despite the risk, there is nowhere he'd rather be.

Globulators at the ready, he and Harlan start after Princess Nnnn and the others, but the toe of Welfy's left foot clips a rock and he stumbles forward. Struggling to maintain his balance, he bumbles into a shadow-thicket, a coiled darkness that presses his arms to his sides, and then out into bright light where he slams into a set of shelves.

He's just come up the basement steps at the back of Gramercy Deli, clutching a bottle of Windex as if it's a gun.

And sitting on an upturned milk crate, waiting for him: an elderly man he's never seen before.

26

RUNNING HEADLONG INTO a set of metal shelves can be painful.

"Ow, ow, ow, ow, ow!"

"You're bleeding," the elderly man says, and points at a gash on Welfy's forearm.

"Ow! Who are you and how—ow, ow!—did you get in here?" The question reminds Welfy. Ignoring the cut on his arm, he looks to the front of the deli, expecting to see smashed windows, shattered glass. But the windows are intact. Except for the mess he made running into the shelves, and the mysterious old guy, everything in the deli is as it should be.

"You are wondering," the elderly man says, "why the store hasn't been damaged by those young men with less than friendly intentions? It's thanks to that resourceful friend of yours, Sandra Zwerling. She secured the aid of the two Original Rays at whose restaurant you recently dined. The Rays' hoodlum-tracking app enabled them to arrive here before any damage had been done. It was they who convinced the hoodlums to run away if they cared for their own well-being. They then contacted me. Now," with a smile of infinite patience, the smile of someone used to knowing things others do not, "would you like to guess who I am?"

"Actually, I'd like to get back," Welfy says, gesturing at the basement steps. But the elderly fellow hoists himself upright and creaks toward him, a red, spiral-bound notebook in his hand. "No way. Morton?"

The old man dips his head in acknowledgment. "Yes, it is I, Morton."

Welfy's thoughts reel to earlier times: to when he first met his boss and guessed him to be in his mid-thirties, to his then noticing the deep lines in Morton's forehead and around his mouth, the unmistakable signs of Morton aging unnaturally quickly.

"But how?" Welfy says.

"I'm 1,143 years old," Morton explains, "give or take a decade."

"Yeah, but—"

"You saw me as you needed to see me," Morton says. "The truth of things often reveals itself slowly. But I know all about you, Welfy. I know more about you than you know about yourself. I always have."

"You can see what most people can't," Welfy says, almost in a whisper. "You're psychic."

"Um, no. I am Princess Nnnn's great-grandfather."

My chancing into Gramercy Deli and asking for work. Morton offering me a place to sleep. The portal. The Brundeedle prophecy. It's all connected. I knew it. Sort of. Didn't I sort of know it?

"The prophecy. You're the one who—"

"Again, I must say *no*. I'm Princess Nnnn's *other* great-grandfather. From the father's side of the family. I am here as what you might call a gatekeeper. I've been waiting for you. We have all been waiting for you—Brundeedles, select Earthlings, and the last of the Gunselzumps, by whom I mean my wife. I believe you suspected something was different about her? Her real name is Laaayaaaaaaaaaaaaaaaaghghghghsosososososo, but we call her Laya or Elle, for short. I have some family photos if you'd like to see."

Welfy eyes the basement steps. "Maybe another time,

okay? 'Cause right now I really have to—"

Morton, however, won't be put off. He scrolls through the pictures on his phone, the same ones Welfy saw in Morton and Elle's bedroom: the couple at the Statue of Liberty, the Brooklyn Bridge, the bandshell in Central Park. Except in these photos, Elle isn't wearing her hair like a rigid helmet. In the middle of her forehead is a mouth—a *second* mouth.

"That's why her voice didn't sound like it was coming from her mouth," Welfy murmurs. "Her regular mouth, I mean. It was coming from her forehead mouth."

Morton nods. "Obviously she's younger than I am," he says.

A two-mouthed Gunselzump isn't as startling to Welfy as it once might have been. "Your notes," he says, indicating Morton's red notebook. "I go down the basement steps sometimes and nothing happens. All that horoscope stuff. You keep tabs on the stars 'cause they'll tell you when the portal will open and when it won't, right?"

"I should confess," Morton says. "I don't know the first thing about astrology or, for that matter, astronomy. The vagaries and mysteries of the celestial realms are fairly vague and mysterious to me."

Morton opens the notebook, shows Welfy that page after page is covered in doodles—Morton♥Laya, Morton & Laya Forever.

"Wait. So you don't know how the portal works?" Welfy asks, unbelieving.

"Not everything can be readily explained, Welfy. Just as there are some paths in life that a person cannot or will not go down, so it is with what you call the portal. It is only for those it is for, if you know what I mean."

"I don't, no. I definitely do *not*."

"I'm not technologically inclined," Morton says with a shrug. "But I've no doubt that a certain Anthos at the Dine-O-Mat can enlighten us about your portal, should we have a chance to visit him."

"The *who* at the *what?*"

"Precisely. For most of your life, Welfy, you have mistakenly believed a small part of reality—this universe—to be the whole of it. But imagine reality as a loaf of sliced bread. Now imagine that each individual slice is a universe. One slice contains this galaxy, the Milky Way, etc. Another slice contains Princess Nnnn's galaxy. Yet another slice contains galaxies you may or may not ever visit. This entire loaf of bread—reality—is what we call a multiverse. And as you have recently discovered, Welfy, the universes that make up the multiverse are perforated. When a person passes through a perforation—you enjoy calling it a portal—that person finds himself in a different slice of reality. Gramercy Deli, for example, is the perforation from this universe to Princess Nnnn's universe. The Original Ray's pizza shop where you dined with your friends is a perforation to another universe. Other Original Ray's shops are perforations to yet more universes, as are several corner groceries and one Starbucks."

"The door," Welfy says. "The one I saw in Original Ray's exactly where the deli's basement steps would be. *That's* how they got those futuristic-looking weapons."

"The Original Rays not only protect disadvantaged New Yorkers from corporate bullies of local origin, they also guard against bullies from other universes."

Welfy's eyes again slide toward the basement steps. "Okay, but why are you telling me this stuff *now?* I mean, you can school me about multiverses and dine-o-whatevers after I help Princess Nnnn, 'cause the chain of events that led me to you and the portal—from my running away when I did to my tripping into the basement carrying peas . . . what does any of it matter now? It *happened* and I need to get back to the Brundeedles. We're about to attack Craetella, and whether or not I can really help, I don't know, but I have to at least try."

"Oh, you believe that you *can* help," Morton says, "and you believe it because others believe. But there are no guarantees, Welfy. The prophecy was unfortunately vague. It said that you would lead the Brundeedles out of Woe Time but not whether you would lead them to victory or to annihilation."

"I understand the risk." Welfy positions himself at the head of the basement steps, breathing deeply, gearing himself up.

"One last bit of news, if I may," Morton says. "Your biological mother, Welfy. Her name is Rae. And she is alive. Rae: R-A-E. Do you understand?"

"Why would you say *that*?" Welfy's voice is tight, almost a growl. His hand is at the folded papers Harlan gave him. "I saw her obituary. Hers and my father's."

"That was a mistake, a misprint. Only your father perished that sad day."

Welfy shakes his head, hard and fast, as if rattling Morton's words around in his skull to smash all meaning out of them.

My mother is not alive. Can't be. I would've found her.

"Liar!" he shouts, and runs down the basement steps, passing through the darkness of the stairwell, emerging into—

The basement.

No. No no no! It has to work! It's going to work!

Welfy sets the light bulb swinging on its wire; shadows loom and slide over the room. He bounds up the steps, back into the brightly lit deli, where Morton stands as before.

"Liar!" he shouts again, and races once more down the stairs, hearing only the sound of his footfalls and his own breathing until he steps out into the Coringa region, about to face the most momentous challenge of his challenge-prone life.

27

WELFY EMERGES FROM a dilapidated Tryndian warehouse, a remnant of the old Tryndian city for which the Ceparids have no use. he is inside the Ceparid metropolis, Craetella's stronghold. Huddled a little distance off: Harlan, Nnnn, Ffff, Bloob, Pogg, and the others.

"You can't keep going off alone to play the hero," the prince scorns at Welfy's approach. "It threatens our ability to function as a team, a military unit."

"Funny, *you* talking about teamwork," Welfy says.

"What does that mean?" Ffff demands. "You don't like my attitude? The savior of the Brundeedles would like to do something about my attitude?"

"Now's not really the time to be—" Bloob interjects.

"Why're you such a tremendous jerk?" Welfy asks the prince. "I never did anything to you."

"No fighting," Pogg says. "We need all of our energy and concentra—"

"And despite what you think," Welfy continues, "I don't want to take your place as leader of the Brundeedles, and I'm not the kind of guy who'd try to sniggle someone else's wife even if I liked her and I knew what sniggling *was!*"

"No," Ffff says, "you're so humble and magnificent, you could never admit to doing anything wrong."

"I didn't say that."

Harlan taps Ffff on the arm. "You have issues, prince. I'm

not flying with you anymore." He looks at the others. "I call someone else's spaceship next time."

"Everyone shut up!" Princess Nnnn pleads, and looks to Pogg as if to say *continue*.

"I will take the right flank," Pogg says. "Ffff will take the left and Bloob will take the middle, as planned. I need not tell anyone that we are greatly outnumbered, that odds are we will not live to see another rising of the Yugmuffin moon."

Bloob pats Pogg on the back. "Way to pump us up. Real good." He raises a fist in the air. "Let's annihilate these goo-heads!"

The Brundeedles splinter off into three columns. Pogg leads one into the shadows on the right side of the street. Ffff leads another into the shadows on the left. Bloob and the rest march down the center of the dim roadway. Weapons at the ready, the three Brundeedle columns move steadily, cautiously forward, penetrating deeper and deeper into the Ceparid metropolis, every step decreasing their chances of making it out alive. They round a corner, holding their formation, and continue with stealth down the street. What was once a bustling Ceparid city, with crowded cafés and restaurants on every block, now appears deserted.

Prince Ffff squints, suspicious of the empty streets. "This is too easy," he says.

A Brundeedle peers down an alley and sees—

A Ceparid doing push ups.

Or does he? Because the alien is gone.

Harlan sweeps a glance over a café and sees—

A Ceparid pouring itself a drink behind the bar.

Or does he? In a blink, the alien is gone.

"Maybe Grrrrmmmph made a mistake?" Welfy ventures.

"He doesn't make mistakes," Princess Nnnn says. "Homing NuNus don't make mistakes."

They turn onto a wide avenue and fan out in front of the Tryndian palace. Most heads turn to Prince Ffff for a signal, although several turn to Welfy. The prince clears his throat.

"Yeah," Welfy says to those looking at him; he indicates the prince, "you should . . . you know."

All heads turn to Ffff. After a moment of quiet, maybe the last quiet moment any of them will ever experience, the prince gives the nod and everyone opens fire, blasting palace doors and windows.

Glass flies, masonry crumbles.

Rushing into the palace behind their bombardment, Welfy, Harlan, and the Brundeedles enter a large, open room with a vaulted ceiling. Thick dust hangs in the air, rubble crunches underfoot. Only hours before, Craetella was birthing her newest soldiers in this very room. But now the room is vacant and the sole remnant of the Ceparid queen is a dark stain on the floor.

"Deserted city," Prince Ffff mutters. "Abandoned palace." Then he realizes: "Everybody out! It's a trap. Out out out!"

YUGMUFFIN MOON

28

ETREAT IS IMPOSSIBLE. Out every broken palace window, every splintered door, the Brundeedles can see Ceparids standing rubbery shoulder to rubbery shoulder, with weapons aimed and ready to fire.

Welfy and Harlan look out at the enemy, then at each other, not wanting to believe.

This is it? This is the end?

One of the Ceparids starts to shake and screech. Other Ceparids join in with screechings of their own, and pretty soon all of them are doing it, heaving with Ceparid laughter. It's an ugly sound—disdainful, audible snot.

"What's so funny?" Bloob shouts. "You want to hear something *funny?*" He sends a torrent of Rador-Blood out a window at the enemy, but before reaching its intended target—

The Ceparids attack the Tryndian palace. A Sticky Orble cannonballs through the front door, pulling up three Brundeedles before exploding.

Surrounded, the Brundeedles retaliate with ferocious urgency, everyone deathly serious except Bloob, who fights with his usual glee, crying "Yaw! Yaw! Yaw!" as he runs the length of the room, sending Rador-Blood out at the Ceparids through every blasted opening.

Welfy and Harlan hunker beneath a window, popping up to shoot at the enemy, then ducking down for cover. With one hand, Welfy works his Globulator, using his other to reach into his apron pocket and pull out various weapons and deli foods, most of which he tosses aside. Whenever he pulls a cube-grenade from his pocket, he heaves it at the Ceparids, annihilating a slew of them at a time—as he does now, with Bloob running past and yelling out over the sounds of destruction:

"Yea-ah! Just like making chicken salad at the deli, right buddy! I never feel more alive than when I'm annihilating Ceparids!"

Welfy doesn't have an opportunity to respond; Rador-Blood explodes nearby.

Prince Ffff shouts something, gesturing toward a spiral staircase at the back of the room—a staircase that leads into the darkness of the palace's upper floors. Welfy takes one look at the stairs and—

The deli.

He hopes that's where the stairs lead anyway, because much of the Tryndian palace is on fire and retreating to its upper floors doesn't seem like the greatest idea.

"Let's go, let's go!" Ffff shouts, dodging thickets of flame and the pull of Sticky Orbles as he progresses toward the staircase. He urges his soldiers upward, but the first Brundeedles aren't halfway to the top when a Sticky Orble zooms in and blows the entire staircase to nothing.

"Here!" Princess Nnnn cries, clearing debris from an opening freshly made by a Sticky Orble. She's the first to lower herself into it—down through the palace's foundation to a catacomb.

Brundeedles cluster about the opening, which only one of them can fit through at a time, as Sticky Orbles continue to bombard the palace. Welfy, Harlan, Prince Ffff, Bloob, and Pogg are among the last to descend, jumping down in quick succession. Almost every Brundeedle still alive—fifteen in all—is in the catacomb. Panicked, the last two in the palace try to squeeze down simultaneously when—

A huge clap of thunder.

The ground shakes, knocking everyone in the catacomb off their feet. Rocks and dirt and scraps of pipe fall from the palace above.

Silence.

Checking themselves for anything worse than scratches and bruises, Welfy and the others glance up at the two Brundeedles who'd been trying to reach safety; they hang limp.

"The palace must have collapsed," Princess Nnnn says.

Pogg nods into the darkness of the catacomb. "Let's get to the surface. For a little while they will think we're annihilated and we can't lose the only advantage we are ever likely to have."

$$29$$

A VENTILATION GRATE FALLS from a wall inside a deserted Ceparid bar. A Globulator appears in the opening, and behind it, Bloob. No Ceparids anywhere, so he climbs out. Pogg, Ffff, Welfy, Harlan, Nnnn, and the rest of the Brundeedles emerge after him. They check for Ceparids behind the counter, under tables.

"It's possible that Craetella's no longer in the city," Princess Nnnn says.

Prince Ffff grunts, unconvinced. "She's here."

Bloob scopes the place for signs of Craetella, any clue that might lead them to her. "Guys?" he says, at the back door.

Ffff is the first to reach him, to see what he sees: a trail of goo leading down the alley.

"Ten to one that's Craetella's goo," Bloob says.

Ffff drops into the alley and follows the goo trail at a rapid pace, tucked in his battle crouch. The others fall in behind him.

The goo leads them down numerous alleys, between dark, armored buildings, the tops of which are too distant to see. Down alley after alley they go, until more than a few Brundeedles start to think, goo trail or not, maybe they aren't going to find Craetella. Maybe it's just not meant to happen. Maybe they should give up, resign themselves to short lives spent in underground caves, on the run.

"Haven't we been this way before?" Harlan asks.

But just then: the unmistakable chatter of Ceparids.

Nosing out around a building at the corner of a sheltering alley, Bloob and Pogg sight a heavily guarded Ceparid bunker. The guards are relaxed, celebratory, swigging from containers shaped like teardrops and—to judge by their loose-limbed knee-slaps—telling one another hilarious jokes.

"They still think it's over," Pogg whispers. "They think they've won."

"I'll take care of them," Bloob says.

He starts back down the alley, but Pogg stops him.

"Our advantage isn't so great that you can rush into battle alone."

"I wasn't going to just rush in there. I was going to draw fire, give you an opening like Welfy here did the other day."

"It's too much of a risk," Princess Nnnn says.

"Yeah, it's a risk," Bloob admits, "but where's the fun without the risk?" He looks at Welfy. "Right, buddy?"

"Uh . . ." Welfy says.

"There is risk and then there is stupidity," says Pogg.

Bloob's expression darkens for the first time. "We start exchanging Rador-Blood with those guards, the Ceparids outside the palace'll be here in no time and we won't have a chance. When the first Rador-Blood hits, someone's got to be pushing through those bunker doors. I distract them, you guys should be able to surprise them and get through. We have one shot at this."

"Take someone with you," Prince Ffff says.

"Uh uh. I'm enough to create a diversion and you'll need all the fire power you can get."

Bloob hustles off, back the way they'd come, to approach the bunker from a different position.

Worse than being shot at, targeted for annihilation: *waiting* to be shot at and targeted for annihilation.

All wait with muscles tensed, fingers on the triggers of their Globulators.

"What's taking so long?" a Brundeedle asks, though hardly half an Earth minute has passed since Bloob left them. "What's—"

"There!"

Bloob is sauntering toward the bunker, the Ceparids too busy celebrating to notice him until he's in front of them.

"Excuse me?"

The Ceparid chatter stops. So does the drinking.

"Yeah, hi," Bloob says, "any of you flubby-heads see a big, gross, sticky, rancid-smelling queen round here goes by the name of Craetella?"

The Ceparids have no time to gather their gooey wits; Bloob lets fly with Rador-Blood, able to annihilate a dozen of them before the survivors get their weapons in hand and he has to dive for cover.

Bolting from their position, Welfy and Harlan and the Brundeedles storm the bunker, weapons spewing.

A platoon of Ceparids converges on Bloob.

Welfy targets them with his Globulator, but there are too many; they return fire and he shields himself behind a decrepit hover-sled.

Bloob's trapped.

He has to do something. Fumbling in his apron pocket, hoping for a weapon capable of taking out the enemy but not his Brundeedle friend, he risks a view over the hover-sled. Bloob, not more than a cube-grenade's throw away, catches his eye and gives an affirmative nod—a nod of respect and friendship, a nod that says he knows what he's facing and it's all right.

Opening his mouth wide, Bloob yells warrior-fashion and sends Rador-Blood at the Ceparids, who, on cue, empty their weapons at him.

In Bloob's place: nothing but flames.

DINE-O-MAT
VENDING
MACHINE

30

ELFY STANDS AMID the fighting, Globulator held loose in one hand, his other hand still in his apron pocket.

Bloob's gone? Bloob's gone!

Rador-Blood explodes at his feet and Prince Ffff darts past, heading for the bunker. Welfy snaps to attention and chases after Ffff, targeting Ceparids with fresh vigor and newfound hatred.

At the bunker, the prince does away with a couple of Ceparids and busts through the door. Welfy is right behind him. It's hard to see in here, the only light coming through a few open window slats. Under the noise of the raging battle—a constant, wet, squishing sound.

Welfy and Prince Ffff, neither looking at the other, skulk toward the squishing sound with Globulators poised.

Something steps into the light. It's a heck of a lot bigger than both of them put together.

"Marmadillion," the prince says.

Another marmadillion appears. And another.

Instinctively, Welfy shoots at them. Rador-Blood splatters their hides, succeeds only in making them bellow and flick out their tongues in anger.

"Our weapons are useless against them," Ffff says.

"How're we supposed to kill them?"

"We're not. We'll have to get around them somehow."

"Yeah, right." Welfy reaches for what looks like an elaborate water gun tucked under his apron strings: a Nebulizer. "We'll see how useless this is," he says and presses the trigger.

Fog issues from the Nebulizer, floats toward the marmadillions and past them. A portion of the bunker wall disintegrates as the fog drifts out into the night, but the marmadillions are unfazed, apparently the only things around not susceptible to the dangers of the Nebulizer.

"No way!" Welfy cries. "Who's making the rules here?"

The marmadillions close rank around Craetella, a few stalking toward the intruders as Welfy hears a voice, the calm voice of Si Spielgut, Baloney King of New York: "Your head, Deederhoth. Use your head."

Welfy suddenly remembers his earlier run-in with the marmadillions: how he and Harlan had been trapped by one of them, how he'd dug into his apron pocket for a weapon and pulled out a lump of headcheese and flung it aside in disgust and the marmadillions lunged after it, leaving a clear path to the fighters, to safety.

"Here." Welfy shoves his Nebulizer at Ffff and rummages in his apron pocket with both hands. Globulator after Globulator, cube-grenade after cube-grenade—he loads Ffff up with everything that emerges from his apron, rummaging further.

The marmadillions stalk closer, their deadly tongues flicking.

"Which part of 'our weapons are useless against them' did you not understand?" the prince says, annoyed, dropping his armful of munitions on the floor. "If you've got a Sticky Orble cannon in that pocket, then *maybe* . . ."

Welfy pulls a brick of jellied meatstuff from his apron: meat-niblets and spices and chopped onion held together by aspic.

Prince Ffff makes a face. "What is *that?*"

"Headcheese," Welfy explains. "It's made from the edible parts of a pig's head. Si Spielgut kept telling me to use my head. I'm going to use my headcheese, which better be close enough!"

As hard as he can, Welfy throws fistfuls of the meat through the opening left by the disintegrated wall. The marmadillions lurch after the food, punching it, beating it up, chomping on it with their powerful jaws.

"Go!" Welfy shouts, pulling more headcheese—and a banana—from his apron pocket. "I'll hold them off!"

A confused Prince Ffff notices he has a clear path to the goo-lathered Craetella and takes advantage.

Squish. Squish squish. Squish squish squish squish.

Newborn Ceparids slip out of the queen's flesh-mouth even now. The prince lifts one of the slobbery lips and thrusts a backpack full of cube-grenades under it.

"Take cover!" he yells, pulling Welfy from the bunker. "Take cover! Move! Move!" he shouts at Harlan, Nnnn, and the others battling Ceparids outside Craetella's hideaway.

Seconds take lifetimes to pass.

An ear-throttling boom.

A storm cloud of fire and stone and smoke.

Earthlings and Brundeedles alike fall face down, arms covering their heads for protection, and lie still until the thunk and clang of destruction is no more and debris has stopped hailing from the sky. Earthlings and Brundeedles alike lift their heads.

Only the bunker's ruined foundation remains. Flames tongue the rubble. A few marmadillions stumble about, discombobulated, but there's not a Ceparid in sight.

Shocked quiet.

Princess Nnnn looks at Welfy, her eyes twinkling. Pogg grins. Welfy has never seen the kid even come close to a smile before. The grinning is contagious, spreading from one Brundeedle to another as the realization comes over them: they annihilated Craetella.

31

ONE RISING OF the Yugmuffin moon later.

The old Brundeedle capital, Zalyx, is an above-ground, war-ravaged city. Once the pride of the race, with its lofty spires and efficient public transportation system, once the center of business and pleasure for many throughout the galaxy, it has become a NothingTown, a relic of the great metropolis it used to be. No Brundeedle has set foot in Zalyx for many revolutions of the Toda sun.

Until now.

In one of the few remaining buildings, in a ballroom formerly used for lavish affairs held in honor of government officials, the Brundeedles enjoy their newfound freedom for the first time, giving full expression to the relief that comes from knowing Craetella will never again be a threat. Jubilant, they mill about, goblets of muddy drink in hand. The youngest among them run around, playing tag and squealing with delight, their fun more deeply felt because, although they don't completely understand the reasons for it, they have never seen their elders so relaxed.

At one end of the hall, Prince Ffff and Welfy stand on a dais surrounded by soldiers. Princess Nnnn is there with her brother Raoul. So are Harlan, Grrrrmmph, and Pogg.

"I'm not sure what to say," Prince Ffff remarks, looking mildly perturbed.

"How about 'we owe you a very great debt,'" Princess Nnnn suggests, leaning in to kiss Welfy on the lips.

Prince Ffff's expression turns sour.

"Hey, *she* kissed *me*," Welfy says.

"Yes, of course," Ffff says. "I suppose you think you're entitled to a great many privileges now."

Welfy tries to interrupt.

"Please do not thrill me by speaking," the prince continues. "Obviously, I'm overjoyed that Craetella has been annihilated and our galaxy restored to us. But this doesn't mean that I will let you sniggle my wife. Nor does it mean that I must actually like you."

Talking stops. Concerned, troubled faces. Welfy doesn't know what to do.

"However . . ." Prince Ffff says, which is all he gets out before a murmur passes through the hall, the revelers part, and a Ceparid straggles into view. It lifts its Globulator, aims and—

Keels over, dead.

As if nothing happened, Brundeedles return their attention to Welfy and the prince.

"However," Ffff resumes, his scowl fading, "I have learned to like you. I realize that I'm not always the easiest Brundeedle to get along with."

"Very true," Princess Nnnn interjects lovingly.

"A xcl̲ m̲lg m̲lgaiol̲," Raoul says, inducing a general chuckle.

"Yes," the prince smiles. "And I have been unfair to you, Welfy Deederhoth. For that, and for my rudeness, I apologize." The prince's eyes are moist with sincerity. "Friend, prophesied one, I thank you. I thank you so very, very much."

Accompanied by a cheer, Welfy and the prince shake hands. Brundeedles pat Welfy on the back, ruffle his hair, punch him approvingly on the arm.

"Without Craetella," Grrrrmmph informs Harlan, who's winking at various females, "her domesticated marmadillions will revert to their wild life in Coringa and be as threatening as typical marmadillions—no more, no less. As for Ceparids, in a short time we will be rid of them. They will die out, any threat of annihilation will die with them, and we can get back to the business of repopulating our cities."

"Sounds like a plan," Harlan says, tipping an invisible hat to a passing Brundeedle beauty.

Prince Ffff lifts his goblet high in the air and the ballroom quiets. "Let us not forget those lost in battle! Those whose courage and valor made our victory possible! Let us never forget!"

Goblets are raised, their muddy contents swallowed down.

How, Welfy wonders, *could anyone possibly forget?*

The Yugmuffin moon has set and risen again, but the celebrations show no sign of flagging. Welfy strolls through the ballroom, Brundeedles frequently stopping him to ask if he'll do "that thing" with his apron for old time's sake. And no matter what emerges from his pocket—baloney slice or Globulator—the Brundeedles laugh and applaud and clamor for the item.

Tossing a radish for a crowd to wrestle over, Welfy sights a staircase carved into a stone wall. Whether or not anyone else sees the stairs that ascend into darkness, he doesn't know. He goes in search of Harlan, finds him talking with a female Brundeedle.

"I want to show you something," Welfy says.

"Does it have to be now? I'm kinda busy."

"Has to be now."

Harlan whispers in the Brundeedle's ear, causing her to giggle, and follows Welfy to the staircase.

"What?" he says. "You telling me this leads . . . ?"

"I'm pretty sure, yeah."

"How do you know?"

"I don't. Only one way to find out."

After a silence, Harlan sighs. "I'm not much good at valedictions, Welf."

"Huh?"

"Valedictions. It means 'acts or instances of bidding farewell.'" Off Welfy's look of incomprehension: "I'm not going back. What do I have to go back to? There, I'm just another kid living on the streets. Here, I helped save an entire species. You could stay too, you know."

Could I?

Welfy considers it. "No," he says finally, "there's something I've got to get back to."

"Yeah?"

"Morton said my mother's alive, that the obituary you found was a misprint. He said she's an Original Ray. At first I thought he was making it up, but why would he? That was just me being surprised and maybe even scared. I mean, my mom's alive and all this time I've thought she was dead? Anyway, I'm not sure I disbelieve Morton as much as I did when he first told me."

"If you see Sandra, you'll explain things to her?" Harlan asks. "Tell her I said goodbye?"

Welfy nods.

"Stop in every once in a while, Welf. I'd hate to think our friendship'll go down the tubes just 'cause we're in different galaxies."

Again Welfy nods. His mouth no longer seems to work. It's kind of awkward, this parting.

"Showing emotion has never been our strong suit, Welf."

Harlan pulls his friend close, and for the first time Welfy experiences how good it feels to be comforted by another person, to just be held. Then Harlan threads away through the crowd, never once looking back.

A quiet minute with Nnnn would be nice, just the two of us, after everything we've been through.

This doesn't seem likely, however. The princess is always occupied, always in Raoul and Prince Ffff's company, always at the center of some group or other. It's as if, with the war ended, the administrative responsibilities of the royal couple as heads of state have already begun.

Part of Welfy wants to go up to every Brundeedle and say his goodbyes. But he knows that if he does, he'll never leave.

Probably better, probably easier for everyone, if I just go. Let the Brundeedles remember me as the mysterious kid who fell from the sky wearing a dirty apron to land in sticky goo, who one day took his dirty apron and vanished as suddenly as he appeared.

He indulges in a final look around the ballroom: at Pogg and Grrrrmmph; at Prince Ffff and Princess Nnnn; at Raoul, who's watching him, a serious expression on his face. The youngster seems to have an inkling of what Welfy's up to; he raises a hand and waves. It's the gesture of someone still very much a child, a grateful child, yet in it Welfy sees the melancholy understanding he associates with world-weary adults, with those who have lived long enough to experience too much personal devastation.

He raises a hand to Raoul, in greeting and farewell, and not without regret starts up the staircase. Darkness overwhelms him. He feels pressure around his ribcage, hears only the sound of his footfalls, then—

Steps out into Gramercy Deli. No hint of Morton anywhere. The metal shelves with their boxes of Tide and Cascade are in perfect order. It could be any old night at the deli, no different from a thousand others.

Welfy lies down on his cot and, fully clothed, with all the lights burning, falls asleep.

32

SAVING A POPULATION from extinction requires a great deal of physical and mental energy. It can tire out even the greatest of heroes. So deeply does Welfy sleep the next morning that he doesn't hear Morton unlock the deli's front door at 5:50 a.m. Nor does he hear Morton putter about the store for the next several hours. A little after 10:00 a.m., his eyelids flutter open. His boss is sitting on a stool next to his cot.

"A hearty congratulations," Morton says. "In honor of the prophecy's fulfillment to the good, which I assume is the case since you've made it back here, Gramercy will remain closed for the day. Why don't you change clothes and wash up? We have an important matter still to tend to."

In the bathroom, Welfy splashes water on his face and arms, dries himself with paper towels, and exchanges his battle-stained wear for clean jeans and a T-shirt. He carefully folds his deli apron, which he carries along with his dirty clothes back out to the deli proper.

"Before I forget," Morton says, "your friend Sandra wanted me to give you this, so you can keep in touch." A Post-It note. With Sandra's phone number, home and email addresses written on it. "Don't misunderstand, Welfy," Morton says. "You'll always be welcome, both here and at my home, and you can stay with me as long as you wish. But my hunch is that you'll want to spend some time getting to know your mother. I suggest you gather your things. I doubt you'll be coming back—not for a little while, at any rate."

"We're going to see my mother . . . now?"

"Why not?"

"I don't know. I just thought . . ."

What, that I'd have time to prepare? Been preparing my entire life.

"Your mother," Morton explains, as Welfy packs his few belongings into a white plastic trash bag, "is now a high-ranking member of the Original Rays gang, but when she became pregnant with you, she and your father had just ascended from apprentice status to their first year as combat-ready members. No Original Ray is supposed to start a family until he or she has been militarily active in the gang for five years. By such time, it is believed, members will fully understand what's required of them and thus be able to balance those responsibilities with the demands of family life. Your mother, uncertain what would happen if her pregnancy was discovered, hid her condition by volunteering, with your father, for an outreach mission tothe NC15 nebula. Before they returned to active, local duty, your mother gave birth to you. I happen to know, Welfy, that no parents have ever loved their newborn son more than your mother and father loved you. Initially, after your birth, they were prepared to admit to the highest-ranking Original Rays that they'd broken the rules, and they were prepared to accept demotion. But they ultimately decided against this—not for their careers, but because they loved you. Those were particularly tumultuous times; in an effort to destabilize the Original Rays, members' families were being targeted by a ferocious alien population that shall remain nameless. Your mother and father rightly feared that with two Original Rays as parents, not only wouldn't you enjoy a stable, nurturing homelife, you likely wouldn't live to adolescence. And leaving the Original Rays altogether wasn't an option for them. Once a member, a person can't ever truly leave the Original Rays. Several have tried; all have been annihilated by enemies they'd fought against while in the gang. So to protect you, Welfy, and wishing a better life for you than the one they were capable of providing, they told no one of your existence and secreted you away to Family Services. Eventually, the danger to members' families diminished to what must unfortunately be called 'more acceptable' levels. When the highest-ranking Original Rays and Brundeedle powers-that-be learned of your birth— and only the highest-ranking Original Rays knew that The One would be born to a member of their number—there was little we could do. Your Family Services file had never been digitized and it was no longer at the office to which you'd been brought as an infant. We could only wait and pray that you would one day present yourself. Now, if you're ready?"

"Hold on."

Welfy slides the package of Huggies diapers out from under his cot, pulls the box of Ritz crackers from amid the diapers, and then the frozen OJ concentrate container from the box of crackers. He removes his roll of cash from the OJ container and stuffs it in his pocket.

"Ready."

Belongings in hand, including his deli apron, he follows Morton to the front door.

Gramercy Deli: one of New York City's last holdouts from a less corporate era, a humble-seeming establishment, yet so much more than an oversize shoebox filled with meat-stuff, cheesestuff, and other stuff.

"Goodbye," Welfy says to the refrigerators that house a limited supply of sodas, juices, energy drinks, and bottled waters. "So long," he says to the freezer with its ice creams and frozen pizzas. "Adios," he says to the sandwich counter, the shelves crowded with detergents, paper towels, canned soups and vegetables. "Later," he says to his little alcove with its cot and shower curtain.

In the taxi uptown, he doesn't ask where they're going, too busy wondering if he'll recognize his mother when he meets her, if he'll see himself in the shape of her eyes, her nose.

What if she she doesn't like me? What if I don't like her?

"Being The One," Morton says, "you are not alone."

"Huh?"

"There are many prophesied ones, from worlds throughout the multiverse. Have you ever asked yourself what happens to the prophesied ones after they have successfully fulfilled their prophecies?"

"Um, no."

"Of course you haven't. Ah, we've arrived," Morton says, seconds before the taxi stops. On the sidewalk, he holds open the Dine-O-Mat's front door, allowing Welfy to precede him inside. "After prophesied ones have successfully fulfilled their prophecies, they come here," he explains. "The diners you see? Some of them *are* just regular customers—people needing a quick bite before getting on with their day. But more than several . . . think of them as the Welfy Deederhoths of other galaxies, other universes." Morton extends his arms to take in the whole of the Dine-O-Mat, the vending machines that offer everything from apples to zabaglione. "We are standing in an employment office for all prophesied saviors seeking work after they have fulfilled their prophecies. Worlds in trouble advertise their need for such saviors through the vending machines. Each world has a specific letter-number combination. For example, you won't see E4 in any of the machines because it's a world currently enjoying a prolonged peace. By selecting a particular item—a chicken wrap with the letter-number combination of L11, say—a savior signals his or her willingness to take on that specific job. Representatives are sent by the world in need. Negotiations entered into. Agreements struck."

What does any of this have to do with my mother? "They all look human," Welfy says.

"Assimilation something or other. Completely reversible . . . most of the time."

To Welfy's left, customers wait in line to consult with a busboy, each customer carrying . . .

Aprons.

Morton inclines his head toward the busboy. "That's Anthos, resident apronologist."

Anthos hunches over a plastic gray tub, concentrating hard on its contents. Maneuvering closer, Welfy gets a view inside the tub, whose interior sides give off a curious light. An apron is spread flat at the bottom of the tub. Embedded in the apron's fabric: what looks like a complex electronic circuit. Anthos' fingers are capped by some kind of high-tech thimbles, each with a telescoping, articulating arm as thin as a sewing needle protruding from it. Anthos manipulates these tiny mechanical arms, tinkering with the apron's circuit.

"What most of us think of as technologically advanced, Anthos considers the stuff of children," Morton says. "His is an intriguing personality indeed, and one day perhaps the two of you will chat, but right now I think you might prefer to say hello to that young lady over there."

Across the room, a woman stands at attention, staring at

them—as if she had risen to her feet when Welfy and Morton entered the Dine-O-Mat but found herself unable to move further.

That's her?

Welfy doesn't yet recognize himself in her features. Nor does he experience the outpouring of love he had expected, the impatience to fling himself into her arms. The actual, physical presence of the woman whose embrace, more than any other, he's so often imagined would mean "home" has rendered him awkward, nervous.

"You going to be okay without me?" he asks Morton.

After all this time. Stalling.

"I hope so. I do seem to have managed for 1,143 years."

"Yeah, I guess. Thanks, Morton. For everything."

"You know where I'll be."

Welfy moves slowly toward his mother, but partway across the Dine-O-Mat, he turns and looks back. Si Spielgut, dressed in a deli apron, with ghostly jar of relish in hand, is hovering beside Morton. The Baloney King raises his relish into the air, as if making a toast in honor of Welfy Q. Deederhoth, meat purveyor, world savior.

What does a kid say to the mother he's always longed for? How express everything he feels? Everything he's *ever* thought and felt about his birth parents, himself, the three of them apart and together?

I can't. It's impossible.

Maybe. But Welfy is now standing in front of his mother, both of them shy, and he has to say something.

"Hello," he says.

Anthos: An-thoss or An-those, depending on your mood.

Brundeedle(s): Brun-DEE-dul. "Brun-" as in "Brun for your lives!" And "-dul" as it sounds in "needle."

Ceparid: SEP-uh-rid. "Sep-" as in "*Sep* away from the spaceship, nice and slow." And "-rid" as in "I'm going to rid the universe of gooey aliens for all time!" The plural is pronounced "SEP-uh-ridz."

Coringa: Core-RING-uh.

Craetella: Cray-TELL-uh.

EeEEecheE: The important thing to remember with Ceparid vocabulary is volume. Capital letters signify shouting. Lower case signifies a more conversational decibel level.

EeeiiiIIIkeIeIeI Annihilation Ray: The first word sounds exactly as it looks.

Gunselzump: GUN-sul-zump.

Marmadillion: MAR-muh-DILL-yin.

Moons of Pyron: Pie-ron. Each syllable is of equal emphasis, as in, "Hey, don't eat my *pie, Ron!*"

Pogg: Never pronounced "paw-guh-guh," since the second 'g' is silent. Rhymes with bog, cog, dog, fog, hog, jog, log, and most if not all things "-og."

Toda: TOE-duh. Rhymes with "soda." As in "What's that on your foot?" "That's my *toe! Duh!*"

Tryndian: Trin-DEE-in.

Yugmuffin: YUHG-muff-in. A common mistake is to pronounce this as "yoogmuffin."

Zalyx: ZAY-licks.

While I hope that readers find *Welfy Q. Deederhoth: Meat Purveyor, World Savior* entertaining, the funny parts of this book are not meant to make light of the issues faced by youth and runaways experiencing homelessness—issues I wish were fiction but which unfortunately are not. Nor are they entertaining.

If you know someone in a challenging family situation who could use advice or emotional support, or if you are interested in learning what you can do to help people in need, please exploit the internet or your local library—both are great places to find helpful organizations.

On the Resources page at welfyqdeederhoth.com, I have listed a number of organizations that serve unhoused or otherwise vulnerable youth and families. Feel free to suggest important additions to this list when you visit the website. People of all ages—not just adults—have the power to help others. Thanks for caring.

BRUNDEEDLE LANGUAGE KEY

BRUNDEEDLE INTO ENGLISH:

A	A̲	B	C	C̲	D	D̲	E	F	F̲	G	G*	H
I	Z	Y	A	X	W	J	V	B	U	T	K	S

I	I̲	J	ˇJ	K	L	L̲	M	M̲	O	R	U	X
C	R	L	Q	P	O	D	M	N	E	F	G	H

ENGLISH INTO BRUNDEEDLE:

A	B	C	D	E	F	G	H	I	J	K	L	M
C	F	I̲	L̲	O	R	U	X	A	D̲	G*	J	M

N	O	P	Q	R	S	T	U	V	W	X	Y	Z
M̲	L	K	ˇJ	I̲	H	G	F̲	E	D	C̲	B	A̲

BRUNDEEDLE KLHG

C MLHG FMJAG*OJB KOG

SLOFF FRIEDBAUM LR ZALYX AH CGGOMKGAMU DXCG MCMB BRUNDEEDLES ILMHALOI GL FO AMKLHHAFJO: GL FIOOL CML LLMODGAICGO MARMADILLIONS.

"A ULG GXO ALOC RILM CRAETELLA, GXO CEPARID ˘JFOOM," FRIEDBAUM OCKJCAMOL GL *GXO KLHG*. "HXO GICAMOL HLMO MARMADILLIONS GL FO XOI UFCILH. GXOB LALMG DLIG* LFG GLL DOJJ CH UFCILH—AM GXCMG*RFJ RLI GXCG—FFG GXCG GXOB ILFJL FO GICAMOL CG CJJ DCH MODH GL MO."

HLLM CRGOI CRAETELLA'S LOMAHO, SLOFF FRIEDBAUM ICMKOL LFG AM GXO CORINGA IOUALM, DXOIO XO ICMLFRJCUOL GXO LKOMAMU LR C LOOK IICGOI GL JLLG* JAG*O HLJAL VILFML. CJJLDAMU C KCIG* LR

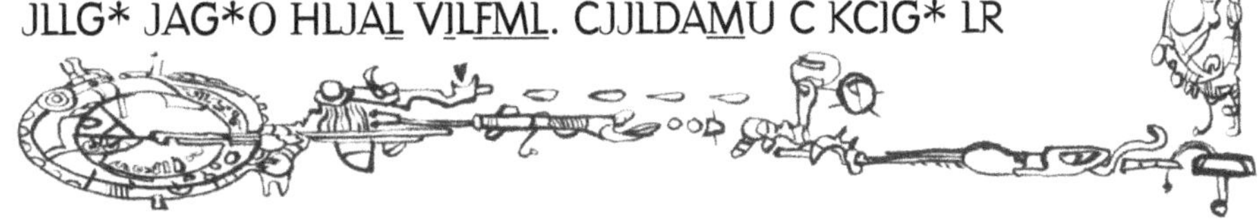

MARMADILLIONS GL ICGIX
XAH HIOMG XO HG*AJJRFJJB
CIICMUOL AG HL GXCG,
DXAJO IXCHAMU XAM,
GXOB ROJJ AMGL GXO
KAG. GXO RAEO ICKGFIOL
FOCHGH ILFJLMG IJAMF
LFG LR GXO KAG OEOM
DXOM HGCMLAMU LM LMO
CMLGXOIH HXLFJLOIH, CML
GXOB ICUOL CML HKCG CG
GXOI ICKGLI.

"DXOM BLFIO LLMO
DAGX GXCG FMFOILMAMU
FOXCEALI, DO DCJJ FOUAM
GICAMAMU," FRIEDBAUM
ICJJOL
LLDM GL
GXOM.
AG
DCHMG JLMU FORLIO
XO CKKILCIXOL GXO KAG
GL RAML XAH GICKKOL
MARMADILLIONS AM
GXOAI IFGO, XCIMJOHH
AMICIMCGALMH.

"FB GCJG*AMU
HLRGJB GL GXO IIOCGFIOH
DXAJO GLHHAMU GXOM
HIICKH LR MOCG, A DCH
CFJO GL UOG
AMGL GXO
KAG DAGXLFG
GXOM

KFRRAMU GXOMHOJEOH FK
GL UAUCMGAI KILKLIGALMH
CML GOCIAMU MO CKCIG,"
FRIEDBAUM HCAL. "CH
GAMO DOMG LM, A IODCILOL
GXOAI KCHHAEO, RIAOMLJB
FOXCEALI DAGX GIOCGH
CML KFMAHXOL GXOAI
CUUIOHHAEO LLAMUH FB
DAGXXLJLAMU GIOCGH,
GXO HCMO CH A DLFJL
GICAMAMU C GBKAICJ
KOG. AM CLLAGALM, AR A
DCMGOL GXOM GL JOCIM
GL HLMOIHCFJG, A DLFJL
RAIHG LOMLMHGICGO C
HLMOIHCFJG, CML LMIO
C MARMADILLION XCL
HFIIOHHRFJJB AMAGCGOL
MO, AL IODCIL XAM LI XOI
DAGX MOCG. A XCEO HL
RCI GICAMOL MB GILFKO
LR MARMADILLIONS GL
DLHGJO CML GFMFJO LEOI
LMO CMLGXOI AM C EOIB
IFGO RCHXALM, CML GL
OMLOCIAMUJB JAMO FK
GLUOGXOI LM CMB HGILMU
FICMIX."

FFG DXB CGGOMKG
GL GICAM FOCHGH GXCG
MAUXG CG CMB MLMOMG
KFRR GXOMHOJEOH FK GL
UAUCMGAI KILKLIGALMH

CML GOCI LRR XAH
CIMH CML JOUH?
    "FJGAMCGOJB,"
FRIEDBAUM HCAL,
"A XLKO GL FIOOL
MARMADILLIONS GXCG
CIO MLG CFJO GL KFRR
GXOMHOJEOH FK CML XFIG
BRUNDEEDLES. A DAJJ LL
GXAH FB RAMLAMU GDL
MFGCMG MARMADILLIONS,
LMO MCJO CML CMLGXOJ
ROMCJO. A DAJJ HGFLB DXCG
AM GXOHO MFGCMGH'
FALJLUB—FB DXAIX A
MOCM, DXCG AM
GXOAI KXBHAICJ
MCG*OFK—IOMLOIH
GXOM AMICKCFJO
LR KFRRAMU
GXOMHOJEOH
FK, CML A
DAJJ ICIORFJJB
FIOOL LMJB
MARMADILLIONS
GXCG ICIIB GXAH
MFGCGALM. CH
GL DXB? ML LMO
LOMAOH GXCG
MARMADILLIONS,
DXOM GXOB
IOMCAM JAGGJO,
CIO CFHLJFGOJB
CLLICFJO. AH
CLLICFJOMOHH
MLG OMLFUX LR C IOCHLM?"

BALONEY

CJJ GXO ICUO

WELFY Q.
DEEDERHOTH, GXO
KILKXOHAOL LMO, UCEO
BRUNDEEDLES MCMB
GXAMUH, GXO IXCMIO
RLI C KOCIORFJ CFLEO-
VILFML RFGFIO FOAMU
GXO MLHG LFEALFH,
CML GXCG RLI DXAIX
DO'IO MLHG GXCMG*RFJ.
HLMODXCG JOHH LFEALFH,
CJGXLFUX DO CIO LMJB
HJAUXGJB JOHH GXCMG*RFJ
RLI GXOM, CIO GXO RLLLH GL
DXAIX WELFY AMGILLFIOL FH.

HAM, TURKEY, KNISHES,
SANDWICH ROLLS,
CHICKEN, HEADCHEESE,
BALONEY, ROAST BEEF,
MORTADELLA. UAEOM C
IXLAIO LR CJJ GXOHO, C
MCDLIAGB LR BRUNDEEDLES
DLFJL FMLLFFGOLJB
OCG HEADCHEESE, GXO
FMILMMLM OLAFJO FHOL FB
WELFY AM GXO LOROCG LR
CRAETELLA. GXAH, LOHKAGO
GXO RCIG GXCG ML
BRUNDEEDLE—MLG OEOM

KIAMIOHH NNNN LI KIAMIO FFFF—G*MLDH OCCIGJB DXCG HEADCHEESE AH, JOG CJLMO XLD GL UOG AG. DXAIX JOCLH FH GL CHHFMO GXCG AG AH OCKOMHAEO.

HEADCHEESE XCH FOOM LOHIIAFOL FB EARTHLING HARLAN MILLS, GXO LMO'H GIFHGOL RIAOML, CH "PIG'S XOCL, IXLKKOL EOUUAOH, CML HKAIOH MACOL GLUOGXOI AM C G*AML LR JELLY." FFG BRUNDEEDLES FOAMU MLMO GLL HFIO DXCG C "PIG" AH, LI "JELLY," GXAH LOHIIARGALM XCH JORG FH ICGXOI KOIKJOCOL.

BALONEY, CJGXLFUX AG
GLL ILMOH RILM "PIG,"
AH JOHH MBHGOIALFH CML
ILMRFHAMU GL FH, FOICFHO
XOIO CG JOCHG, HARLAN
MILLS XCH LLMO MLIO
GXCM MOIOJB LOHIIAFO
AG. FHAMU AMUIOLAOMGH
XO IORFHOH GL LAHIJLHO,
FFG DXAIX XO KILMAHOH
ILMO OCIJFHAEOJB RILM LFI
DLIJL, XO XCH RCHXALMOL
C MOD HLIG LR BALONEY—C
BRUNDEEDLE BALONEY,
LAHGAMIG RILM DXCG
AH RLFML LM EARTH. CML
DXOGXOI HARLAN MILLS
RCIG*CUOH GXAH MOCG
FMLOI GXO MCMO BALONEY-
LIKE™ LI BALONEYISH™,
BRUNDEEDLES CKKCIOMGJB
ICMMLG UOG OMLFUX LR
GXO HGFRR.

OBADIAH LLLL (KAIGFIOL)
LOHIIAFOH C KILFJOM
HXCIOL FB UILIOIH
GXILFUXLFG LFI MOGILKLJAH:
"A XCEO GILFFJO GOOKAMU
BALONEY-LIKE KILLFIGH AM
HGLIG*. OEOM GXLFUX BLF
HOO MO DAGX KJOMGB LR
AGOMH GLLCB—XOIO'H C
MAIO DCI LR BALONNAISE
SPREADABLE BALONEY, RLI

AMHGCMIO—
AG DAJJ CJJ
FO ULMO FB
GLMLIIILD."

DXAJO HEADCHEESE AH
C ICIO, ILMRFHAMU
JFCFIB, GXO IOCHLMCFJB
KIAIOL BALONEY-LIKE™ CML
BALONEYISH™ KILLFIGH
CIO OEOIB-BRUNDEEDLE
RLLL. FFG KIAIO CML
FMLOIHGCMLCFAJAGB
CJLMO LL MLG OCKJCAM
GXO OMLIMLFH KLKFJCIAGB
LR GXAH MOCG. KOIXCKH
GXO IOCHLMH RLI AGH
KLKFJCIAGB JAO OJHODXOIO.
KOIXCKH AG AH GXCG
DO AMCUAMO DO CIO
ILMMFMAMU DAGX GXO
LMO DXOMOEOI DO FAGO
AMGL C BALONEY IXAK—
GXCG OXOIOEOI WELFY
DEEDERHOTH MAUXG FO,
XO AH CG GXCG EOIB HCMO
MLMOMG FAGAMU AMGL C
BALONEY IXAK, GLL.

ABOUT THE AUTHOR

A ghostwriter of *New York Times* bestselling YA fiction, the
novel *Static*, and more, Eric Laster lives in Los Angeles,
where he writes fiction and records punk rock.

ABOUT THE ILLUSTRATOR

Max Graenitz lives and works in Germany's Bavarian Alps
as an artist, illustrator, and animator. He has contributed to
projects for Disney, Dreamworks, Jersey Films, Amblination,
and many others.

welfyq.com

www.ingramcontent.com/pod-product-compliance
Lightning Source LLC
Chambersburg PA
CBHW061122100726
47911CB00013B/641